IT'S NOW OR NEVER

THE TAPESTRY OF TIME
BOOK 2

STEVEN TEMPLAR

MYSTERIOUS INK PUBLISHING

It's Now or Never
Book 2 in the Tapestry of Time
By Steven Templar

Copyright 2024

The included playlist features songs selected by the author. All rights to the music belong to their respective creators and copyright holders. No affiliation or endorsement is implied.

Chapter header graphics by Trevor Sutherland.

Playlist

The following is a playlist of tracks that helped shape this story, some even heard by the main character during the course of the novel's events. I include one track sugges-tion. However, listen any way you'd like: before, during, after, never. Or in a few years, in an alternate timeline..

Jellyfish - I Wanna Stay Home
Crystal Bats - Anyone
Com Truise - Brokendata
Mikuni - Nightmoves
Mark Dee - Falkor Flight
Global Communications - 14:31
FM Attack - Timeless
Roosevelt - Ordinary Love
(Chapter 20) Belinda Carlisle - I Get Weak
Andrew McMahon in the Wilderness - Driving Through
A Dream
Carly Rae Jepsen - Roses
OutKast - Prototype
Downtown Binary - Cirrus
Gunship - Black Blood Red Kiss (feat. Kat Von D)
Mark Dee - Nebula
Metric - Now or Never Now
Wild Nothing - Shallow Water
Elvis Presley - It's Now or Never

Author Website : steventemplar.com

A NOTE FROM THE AUTHOR

Hey there. I'm glad you're here. What you are about to read is the continuation of a journey through time and self-discovery, both for many of the characters, and also my writing. I hope you have as much fun reading this as it was to write.

Lots of research went into the historical elements. However, I've taken liberties to enhance the fictional story.

Content wise: This novel would get the equivalent of an American R movie rating, just for language alone. It is packed with scenes of action, some blood, death. And if you feel confused from time to time—that's ok. You're right there with our MC. Thanks again, and enjoy the ride.

PROLOGUE

"Have you noticed anything strange today?" the voice on the other end of the phone asked.

I almost didn't recognize Quinton, my brother from another lifetime. It had been months since I heard from him, despite being tasked as my *guide*—whatever that was supposed to mean.

"He finally speaks. I'd figured you forgot about me," I said.

While living in the unknown for the past year was nerve racking at times, it was a nice break from running for my life. So was the reprieve from the flashbacks of past lives and alternate futures.

"What is today's full date?" That's the Quinton I remember, straight to the point.

"Wednesday, October 1st, 2008—" I stopped tuning my guitar to focus on the call. "*Shit.*"

"Yeah. I thought so." He sighed loudly.

I braced myself against one of the giant speakers in Cartoon Graveyard, the hole in the wall bar I had been calling both work and home the past few months. First came the nausea, my insides churning and grinding against each other like the cogs in an old grandfather clock. Next were the brain zaps, electricity flowing through my head accompanied by an acrid burning smell that made my eyes water. A few mundane visions exploded in my mind; watching the latest episode of CSI, grocery shopping, searching Facebook for a certain... someone.

And then it was over. The pain, the smells, the dizziness—gone. I looked around to find nobody had noticed. Good. That means this was a short one.

"*Woke up*?" Quinton's voice buzzed from the cellphone. Thankfully, I had set it down on the speaker before the dizziness hit.

"Yeah. You ever get used to that?" I groggily shot back. I gently massaged my eyelids, careful not to press too hard. Adjusting to a new timeline was never pleasant—thankfully it's not very common.

"It never feels good, but luckily we only went back one day, I think. Unlike last year," Quinton chuckled.

He likes to get those jabs in when he can. Not like sending the world back from 2014 to 2007 was my choice. I'm still not entirely sure how, but it gave everyone in Tempus a massive headache. Fortunately, it didn't affect a majority of the general population. Or at least it hadn't so far.

"How can you be sure?" I realized I was dripping sweat and grabbed a towel to dry my hair. Much easier after I cut it short, a first in my adult life.

"I woke up earlier today. Pharaoh called me the moment Lotus got a hit that something was askew.

Names I wished I forgot. The past keeps finding a way to make life even more confusing, just when I'm about ready to move on. "Thanks for the heads up," I said sarcastically. "Now I can make sure I watch the same show over again. Have the same dinner again. Go to sleep at midnight alone again."

"You're in luck. You're being summoned. The Tempus Council is sending a car over right now."

If I were drinking something, I'd do a spit take. "Wait —What? A year of radio silence and *now* they decide to bring me in?"

"You know I don't make the rules. I'll be waiting for you when you arrive."

"And what if I say no?" I'm sure Quinton could hear my smirk through the phone.

"I'll tell you about her," he said, devoid of emotion. His response came with no hesitation. Was I that predictable?

Olivia. This must be serious. Any other carrot and I wouldn't take the bait. I stopped pestering Quinton months ago after realizing it was going nowhere. But despite what I told myself, she never left my mind. That feeling I had about her...

I played it cool. "You gotta try harder than that. I've moved on from her. It was nice while it lasted."

A cackle from the earpiece. "Your search history and all the late nights driving around say otherwise."

I pulled the phone away and stomped my foot, then punched the air—I must have looked like a two-year-old throwing a tantrum. I should have figured there was no privacy with these people.

"I'm yours. Give me something?" I whimpered more than I'd like to admit.

"She's alive. That's all you get for now."

Asshole. I looked at my Rolex Submariner, a late birthday gift from Quinton. 8:30 pm. I'd mostly sworn off material things now that I'm not an ultra famous celebrity, but Quinton said these watches keep on ticking through time jumps. "You know, this means my day is going to be different..."

"No need to stick to the script. Trust me, we have a much bigger problem than making sure you pass out alone in that bachelor pad tonight." Oof, he was ruthless sometimes.

I shook my head with a genuine smile across my face. Even though Quinton reminded me of the most stressful night of my life, I missed our conversations. Plus, he was one of the few people I could trust.

"I'll be there with bells on."

The line went dead. I finished packing my guitar, locked it behind the stage, and left a note for the manager. I only played until nine on weekdays because of trivia night. I doubt they'd miss me.

Outside, a light breeze carried the scent of lavender and honey. The moon was already peaking through the clouds, but the warm San Diego sun still lingered in the air. While the weather reports said thunderstorms and tornadoes were nearby, the sky told the story of a cool, peaceful night. At least that's what I kept telling myself while the grey sedan rolled up to the curb.

I wondered how long the car would idle if I didn't make my move. The dark tinted windows gave no clue to who I was playing chicken with. After about a minute, I decided the petty games would only move me further from my goal of laying in my comfy, overpriced mattress as soon as possible. I approached the rear door to a loud *click*—just as I grabbed the handle. Perfect timing.

Inside, the small car was deceivingly spacious and

eerily dark, mostly due to the partition blocking my view of the front cab. The black and grey pleather seats made a satisfying crunch as I settled in the back and the new car smell was pleasant, but strong. The thing about Tempus —they spared no expense. It didn't hurt that they had control over the economy.

The driver peeled out into the street with ease, smoothly dodging cars at a brisk speed until reaching the freeway. After a few minutes, the silence was uncomfortable.

"Hey. You up there. Can you hear me?"

A few seconds later, the divider lowered, exposing my chauffeur for the evening. A bald white man, maybe in his late 40s, focused fully on the road ahead. From the rearview mirror, I saw his face hidden behind a pair of jet-black sunglasses. He wore a dusty old grey suit that matched his bland, unassuming facial features.

My heart skipped a beat. A member of Orchid—the yin to Lotus's yang. When I last saw their leader, Lucian, he was hauled away as a statue next to his partner in crime Alycia. Either things had cooled down or I was being driven to the middle of nowhere for an execution.

"So, uh... where we headed?" I asked.

The driver turned his head, sunglasses peering at me from the mirror, then back to the road while the divider rose, leaving me in darkness. Not a promising start. Hopefully, this would be a quick trip.

CHAPTER 1

The loud thud jolted me awake and alert. Disoriented, it took more than a few seconds to piece together the noise—the driver's door shutting. With a deep sigh, I paused for a moment of gratitude. After being plagued by strange dreams from my life in China centuries ago, *not to mention an alternate future*, I made sure to thank the universe when I had some decent, dream-free sleep. Even if it came at the cost of being sprawled out in the backseat of a stranger's car.

The nap didn't help—Olivia was still fresh on my mind. Thanks Quinton. That weird interaction at the back of the bus. That look in her eyes etched in my brain. She took my number, but I was a total stranger to her. I had so many questions. Who gave me her journal? Who was that bald guy she left with? And the biggest question of all, why did she choose to forget me? I took it personally, despite rationalizing she probably didn't want to be part of some secret time traveling cult. That bitterness is still there, too. With every lead turning into a dead end, the thought of something, *anything*, excited me.

I broke away from the thoughts and took stock of my surroundings. Not getting much from the darkened windows, a quick glance of my watch showed it was two in the morning. My driver must have just left—the partition was down and the front was empty. A yawn escaped my mouth while I stretched the arms and neck of my twenty-two-year-old body—although sometimes it felt much, much older. Even though I've been working out almost daily the past year, and in better condition than when I had a personal trainer in my celebrity days, it was easy to slip into the mindset of my ancient self. Carrying around a few extra decades of memories will do that, I guess.

I opened the door and stepped outside, sand crunching loudly underneath. The sky was nearly pitch black, peppered with stars and satellites spanning the vast nothingness. A burst of cool night air hit my exposed skin, goosebumps forming on my arms. With only a t-shirt and jeans, I was underdressed. Another strong breeze rolled through, bits of sand forcing me to shield my face.

Using my amazing powers of deduction, *and my eyes*, I was somewhere in the desert with nothing in sight for miles, aside from a tiny two pump gas station a few hundred feet away. I wasn't dead yet, so the execution theory was on hold. A desert in the middle of nowhere still seemed like a great place for one—maybe the driver stopped for a snack? Not one to prolong the inevitable, I headed toward the dimly lit snack oasis ahead.

Through the dirty convenience store windows, the driver appeared to be having a conversation. The grime on the rest of the windows made it too hard to see much of anything else.

Another quick survey showed no defining features. Just a run-down building, some pumps, and a small garage, all looking to be in desperate need of repair. I began to wonder why the driver parked so far but stopped myself—I've learned not to question things too much. At least until I need to.

The station door creaked louder than the bell dinging above. Inside the small building, a row of empty refrigerators on the perimeter flanked two aisles of snacks, candy, and knick knacks. A thick layer of dust caked over everything, giving a dull grayish appearance. If anyone shopped here, it must have been years ago. The smell of must caught up to me next, with an unpleasant coughing fit lasting long enough to irritate my lungs.

The sound of a throat clearing pulled my attention to where the driver had stood. "Welcome," a woman in her early thirties greeted me.

I approached the counter and paused, studying the woman behind the smudged plexiglass barrier. My heart skipped a beat.

"Took ya long enough, hun." The woman smiled warmly.

Melissa. The first real support after stepping off the greyhound from Detroit to San Diego. One of the few people that made me feel sane during the chaos of last year. I almost didn't recognize her. The loose leather jacket and jeans were a stark contrast from the apron. Now a strawberry blonde, her locks were up in a bun and with just a splash of makeup, a pinkish glow added to her pale rose complexion. Even her posture and body language were different from the sweet southern girl I remembered.

"Long way from the diner." She winked, lips curling into a devilish grin. "No guitar this time?"

I tried to reply, but something along the lines of "*uhhhh*" was all that came out.

"I know, you weren't expecting to see me."

I shook my head and massaged my forehead, hoping to channel something witty or at least a full sentence. "I went back looking for you. They said you quit and moved."

"I mean, both technically true," she said, biting her lip with a pronounced shrug of her shoulders.

I ran my fingers through my reddish-brown beard—I had finally let it grow longer over the past few months. My nervous habit only acted as a temporary distraction. The relief of seeing a familiar face wore off quickly, turning into the existential fear I had hoped to leave behind.

She looked away, pretending to adjust her jacket before locking eyes again. "I'm sorry about that. Honest, I am." I never noticed how striking her green eyes were. "You mighta guessed by now, but that waitressing gig wasn't my real job."

Heat rushed through. Being deceived was never a great feeling, especially by someone you trusted. "So... can I ask what was or is real?"

She brushed aside a few loose strands of hair, tucking them behind her ear. "I still *am* a southern bell, Texas proud, all of that's true!" She dropped the smile and her tone grew serious. "When we first caught wind of time resetting, Q realized it had to do with you. We knew you originally became a regular at that diner. Sooo, I figured we could keep an eye on you there and at the motel until we figured out what to do next." She looked and sounded genuine, I'll give her that.

"Quite the plan. I don't imagine it worked out too well?" I said with a hint of condescension.

"Yeah, that's on me, kinda," she looked away with a flush of embarrassment. "I was supposed to keep tabs on ya, but I got a lil too helpful. That old banknote you got, sending you to the pawnshop... I didn't think it would lead to all that. You just looked so lost. I was trying to be helpful. It just slipped out."

I appreciated her honesty. It took away some of the anger, but my guard was still up. Throughout my lifetimes, I've learned that trust is a limited and valuable commodity.

"C'mon, I'll make it up to ya with a cup of coffee, on the house. Plus they're waitin." She turned and hit a button near the cash register. Near the far back wall, an empty refrigerator popped open to reveal a dark corridor.

"Wow, do you guys pride yourselves on being overly secretive?" I chuckled.

"Just wait," she said, proudly beaming.

A gentle vibration coursed through the soles of my shoes. Gradually intensifying and reaching my ankles, it climbed my body. Accompanied by a soft rumble, the surrounding noise grew into the loud, thunderous scraping of metal and steel as the vibration became aggressive, causing me to lose balance and grab hold of the counter. I looked over to Melissa, already bracing herself with a knowing smile. She craned her neck to the window, motioning to look.

Darkness partially obscured the dirty stained windows. We were slowly descending into the earth, gas pumps, building, and all. Chunks of earth and sand particles sprinkled and clanked against the walls as we continued sinking, blackening the windows completely. Not normally claustrophobic, I was surprised by the threads of fear shooting within, relieved they faded as the grinding slowed.

Melissa exited the booth and motioned to follow into the dark, secret hallway. She flicked a switch, turning on a series of light blue-tinted bulbs exposing a set of stairs leading further downward. "Let's rock."

CHAPTER 2

"Wow." I was at a loss for words for the second time today.

The steps seemed to go on forever, leading us deeper into the depths below. If I had to guess, we were at least two hundred feet under the desert. Instead of the musty, stagnant air I expected, a strong woodsy scent—like being immersed in a forest after a rainstorm—took my senses by surprise. The long, sterile white hallway took us past several closed steel doors, ending at a set of large frosted glass panels. Now up close, I saw bright flickers of light and a blurred silhouette through the glass.

Melissa peeked over her shoulder with a playful expression, then swiped her wrist over a small square on the wall. The doors glided apart in one smooth, silent motion. "Welcome."

I followed her inside, taking in the large open space. To my left, a giant glass window stood between me and a picturesque, lush expanse of trees with mountains looming in the distance. I crept closer and pressed my hands against the glass, the icy window tickling my palms. Further through the trees, I spotted a young deer drinking from a pristine stream. Where the hell were we?

Gentle pressure on my shoulder brought me back to the room. I turned to Melissa, standing close behind, heat radiating off her. "Beautiful simulation, isn't it?" she said, extending her hand over the vastness. "The smell after it rains is my favorite. It helps me forget I'm cooped up so far down here sometimes."

I rubbed my eyes and backed away from the window. The landscape had distracted me from noticing anything else in the room. A long table accented the center, giving a great view of the thirty monitors lining the back wall. I couldn't help but notice the few laptops scattered on the desk seemed more advanced than the current 2008 models. They would have fit better in 2014 or beyond. The other side of the room had a few lockers and more frosted glass doors.

"Have a seat. They'll be here in just a few," Melissa said, sitting by the desk and kicking out a chair for me. She muttered something about my reflexes after it rolled into my shin.

I shot my own playful, annoyed look. "What is all this?" Now sitting beside her, my eyes darted, bouncing between the screens. The row of monitors ran through a series of images, fueling the distraction. Some showed outdoor shots of areas that looked vaguely familiar, others more private locations with strangers going about their day. Every few seconds, two of the monitors flashed numbers accompanied by a soft beep.

"Glad you could take a nap on the way over," Quinton's voice drifted from my side.

I shifted over to catch the far doors open, Quinton's long grey ponytail brushing across the back of his neck as he approached. His well manicured beard was now more salt than pepper, matching the cream button down shirt draped over a pair of dress pants. His skin looked more wrinkled than I remembered, hard lines etched into the light olive complexion. Behind him, the driver, eyes still covered despite the low lighting.

Melissa waved them over. "Hey Q, I was just showing Jay the ole hideout," she snickered.

Even though it was my name, it was odd to hear her call me Jay like we were old, close friends. While my license reads Jay Biały, the surname from my Polish-Born life, I still feel a connection to *Hagaki*. The nickname I kept from another lifetime, hundreds of years ago in China after I immigrated from Japan—not to mention what eventually became my hip-hop persona. Going by Hagaki made things easier for me, other than the awkward first introductions from my obvious European appearance. Plus getting people to write and pronounce Biały was just as confusing.

Quinton and the sunglass enthusiast sat at opposite sides of the long desk. "Long time, brother," Quinton said with warmth in his voice. "You've been in the dark too long. It's time to get you up to speed."

Brother. I've been calling him that—and it felt true— but hearing it from him was surreal. As if remembering my life in China *and* my alternate celebrity-future wasn't enough, Quinton had a life with me in jolly old England —at least that's what he said. I couldn't remember any of it for the life of me.

I shifted in my seat and crossed my arms. "Finally, the big reveal. Time to learn all the secrets of the universe, right?" I may have come off a bit snarky.

Melissa snorted a quick, breathy laugh. "Yeah, something like that." She turned to her laptop and pressed a few buttons. Most of the large screens changed to the same image. The hazy display on the monitors showed a young woman about my age walking through a rainy downtown city. I couldn't find enough detail to get a sense of where or even when the video was taken. After a few seconds, it looped to show her walking through the same stretch of street.

Quinton pushed himself away from the desk, rolling his chair out to see me and Melissa better. "I know you've been slowly figuring these things out." He dramatically clapped his hands together. "Welcome to one of our monitoring centers!" He extended his hands in a grand gesture, giving the impression of presenting to a crowd.

I heard Melissa sigh and caught a glimpse of her eyes rolling. "So, getting down to business. Lotus's primary job is to watch and identify any changes in the timeline. Or more specifically, the travelers that created them. All this technology helps, but we're instinctually more sensitive to these changes. We are the first ones to realize when it's happened."

"And some of us," Quinton added, pausing to gesture at Melissa, "feel these changes in real time. None of the fun *waking up* that you and I experienced today, Jay."

I nodded, understanding. So far, so good. This is what I had figured. "So you watch for any changes, that's it? What if there is one?"

Sunglasses stood from his seat and walked over to the lockers. "That's where I come in." His voice was airy, but surprisingly human. Last year when I came face to face with one of his partners, I would have sworn they were cyborgs or some kind of clones.

"You've already met Vance," Quinton said dryly. "Things have somewhat stabilized between us and Orchid."

Vance keyed a combination on the locker and pulled out a small black duffle bag before returning to the desk.

Melissa continued her explanation, "Once we've determined the who and the what, we work with our *friends* at Orchid and assist them in tracking down any travelers." I couldn't tell if she was joking or if the disdain was real.

"As Melissa mentioned earlier…" Vance removed a small USB drive from the bag and plugged it into a laptop. "Several of us possess particular gifts. Most of us in Orchid are *drawn to* time anomalies." He clicked around on the computer and several monitors changed to display a series of numbers and graphs, the looping video of the girl still in the center.

"Thanks V," Melissa said. "So, when I see a blip on the timeline like the one today, I narrow down the location and call up my contact. Next thing you know, someone like Vance goes and gets 'em. We bring this person, traveler, to the Tempus Council. The rest, well, *you know*."

I had to laugh. "Not like last year, huh?"

"Last year was inconceivably different," Quinton said.

I propped my elbows on the desk and leaned forward. "I have a suspicion there's a big *but* you're about to drop on me." I almost followed up with a crass joke, almost. If anyone caught my inflection, they didn't show.

"Mr. Hagaki," Vance said, leaning back in his chair until it squeaked. "The red lines on the graphs in front of you represent each instance I've attempted to intercept this woman. Each time I get close, the day begins anew."

I squinted an eye, trying to focus on the gibberish while I let the words sink in. "The day repeats? Like in Groundhog Day?" I relaxed my eyes and looked over at Vance with a grin. No smile from him, clearly not a movie fan. "Are you saying someone else has fucked with the timeline worse than me?"

Unsurprisingly, the man wearing dark sunglasses in the dark room was unphased. "Not yet. You still have the record there. But we've gone through this day for quite some time."

"Okay. And when you don't *intercept* her. What happens then?"

The heads in the room swiveled to each other, passing over me like I was transparent. I tried to read their expressions, each a different shade of uncomfortable.

"It doesn't end well," Quinton said. "If Vance does nothing, we have even less than 24 hours before we're back here again." He looked at a screen displaying the time. "It's just past three in the morning. You have eighteen hours, give or take."

"So that's why you're here, Jay," Melissa chimed in. "We've never seen anything like this. I'll disagree with Vance over there. This jarring repetition to the timeline has the potential to be *even more* disastrous than your extended trip. We have to tread lightly here, one step at a time." She exhaled and reclined in the chair. "And *today* has been the longest *month* of my life. I've been trying everything I can think of. And even worse, I seem to be the only one that remembers every reset while the rest of ya'll are wiped clean after about twenty-four hours. As far as we know, I'm the only person in Tempus that has been living this day over and over and over and—"

"Okay, I get it. I think," I interrupted. "So, why me? Am I the last resort?" I laughed aloud.

I scanned their faces once more, the three of them looking at each other again, until in unison, they each had some variation of "Yes."

CHAPTER 3

"Oh, I almost forgot." Melissa pulled a cellphone from her jacket and handed it through the open window of Vance's car. I chose to sit up front, hoping to learn something from the man. "We can keep in touch better this way, plus it's a 'lil more advanced than what ya have right now," she beamed proudly.

I checked out the phone—compact, silver, and a glossy touchscreen. It was a big change from the flip phone I had grown accustomed to—again. It looked three or four years newer than what was on sale today. "Thanks. How did you..."

Melissa chuckled. "Things take a while to get to market. I figure ya know how to use it, right?"

"Yeah, I was getting sick of T9 texting anyway."

Vance let out a loud cough from the driver's seat. "We do not have much time. Are we ready?"

Quinton appeared beside Melissa and placed a hand on the roof before leaning to the window. "Call me as soon as you get near her. And please, please, *please* do not approach her until I say so."

I struggled to put my hands on my hips in a playful gesture while the seatbelt fought back. "You don't have to tell me twice!" It seemed natural to try to lighten the mood.

Quinton shook his head then stepped away from the car. "Good luck, and keep us updated."

AFTER ABOUT TEN minutes of staring at the endless stretch of dark desert road, I broke the silence. "So, where are we headed?"

If he heard me, Vance did a great job of pretending he didn't. Not moving a muscle, he looked straight ahead, occasionally breaking to check the side mirrors.

"How are you seeing anything with those sunglasses?"

Still nothing. Even when he glanced over, it was like he saw straight through me. I waited another few minutes until the boredom caught up. Might as well listen to some tunes. I fumbled with the radio, searching from station to station for something to pass the time.

My new friend started tapping his fingers until finally speaking. "Do you mind?" Without looking from the road, his index finger found its way to the radio and ruined any chance of fun.

"Hey if we're cooped up in here for who knows how long, you gotta give me something."

"We're getting close. Distractions make it harder to find her."

Finally, something. I would at least try to get something out of this trip.

"So how does that work anyway, the tracking?"

An annoyed sigh from my left. "I just feel it. A pull toward her. It gets stronger the closer I get."

"Makes sense, I guess. Why can't Lotus just go find her? They seem to know enough."

"They can typically pinpoint to a general area, but details and specifics really aren't their thing. And they mostly watch."

Feeling the annoyance in his tone, I staggered my questions. My watch showed it was just before six in the morning, the sun just getting ready to rise. From the sun-worn road signs, we were headed east, creeping into Utah. The surroundings gradually transitioned from lonely stretches of sand into small, rural cities. Although the dark, quiet isolation had its charm, a wave of relief washed over as I finally saw another car on the road.

"How come the day hasn't reset yet? I mean, if this loop thing keeps happening?" I asked.

Vance's head abruptly shifted from side to side as though pulled back to reality. For the first time, he showed some signs of humanity, taking off his sunglasses to massage his eyes. They flickered an eerie glow before being quickly covered.

"From what Melissa is seeing, it occurs around five pm today," he stated without acknowledging what just happened. "The exact time fluctuates depending on when and if I approach her, but either way, we haven't been able to break the cycle."

"So, what's the plan when we find her? Kidnap her? Kill her? Take her out to dinner and a movie?" Maybe I could get this guy to crack a smile.

I was caught off guard to see him looking back, or at least in my direction. The dark lenses blocked his eyes, but not well enough to hide the heat searing behind. "Are you doing a book report?"

"I'm just trying to figure out my role in this. Before today, all I've been told is to keep playing music in that old bar. Stay in California. Don't go looking for the girl I think I'm in love with. All of which I'm not too happy about."

"You know what I'm not happy about? Being stuck with you. Things are finally stabilizing within Tempus after you fucked us over, and I really don't want a repeat."

"I'm sorry I just—"

"You do not get it, do you? This isn't fantasyland, kid. I will not spell it out for you like a video game tutorial." Vance was livid. He kept his composure on the road, but his tone and the vein on his bald head told another story.

I've had plenty of time to think over the past few months. If I were in his shoes, I wouldn't be happy with myself either. Reliving the same seven years over and knowing it, *and* not being able to change anything must have been excruciatingly boring. I didn't want to imagine having to make the same mistakes twice to avoid a paradox or create *time residue,* as they called it. But I didn't do it on purpose and still didn't know *how* it happened.

I paused before responding. "I get it. You're pissed. Most of you guys are. I didn't ask for this and I'm still in the dark. I just want to help."

Vance gripped the wheel, his hands flush of color. He took a deep breath and exhaled loudly. After a few seconds of controlled breathing, he lowered his window, letting in a gust of cool air. The chilly breeze seemed to lower the tension in the car as we rode in silence. He exited the freeway and drove a few more miles until stopping at a red light.

"We're very close. She's somewhere around there." He cocked his chin to the giant sign reading *Zion National Park - 15 miles*. "I need a few minutes to get a better lock on her," he said, pulling into the cozy diner parking lot. He pushed a knuckle into his head, squinting hard enough for me to see through the glasses. "Give me fifteen. Go grab me a coffee. It is the least you can do."

Coffee sounded good, especially with only a quick nap earlier. I swung my feet out the door and planted them on the cracked pavement, stopping to fill my lungs with fresh air from the nearby forest. The first two steps were fine—it was on the third I forgot how to walk. Or my legs decided to stop working, sending me crashing to my hands and knees. I spit on the ground, hoping the vertigo came out with the thick saliva. My heart fluttered while a warm hug blocked out the brisk morning air. I dusted myself off, scraped palms and all, then rose with a painful smile.

"You alright?" Vance yelled out the open door.

He eventually helped me up, leading to a quick chat over coffee. Vance wasn't a man of many words, but he was eager to listen as I described the tumble. It wasn't the first of its kind over the past year. In fact, I had kept note after the third time—today would make it number five. Before heading back to the car, Vance finally broke and gave a quick explanation that didn't make either of us feel better—either I was being tracked or I was tracking someone. Unless I was doing it subconsciously, the former seemed more likely.

The sun now shining its gentle warmth on my skin, it

cast a radiant light on the road and the lush green scenery. I scoffed, realizing the never-ending red light forced me to take in the beauty of the surrounding trees and mountains looming around us.

"I guess I should check-in with the boss." I reached for my shiny new phone and scrolled through the contacts. Over thirty different names populated the list, most of which I didn't recognize.

"Not yet," he said, pressing on the gas after the light turned green. "We still need to—"

The pickup truck must have been going over ninety miles per hour. It slammed into the driver's side, lifting the car up several feet until it crashed back to the ground. Airbags exploded around us sending shards of glass in every direction. An attempt to speak led to coughing out a metallic taste instead. My face was wet, vision blurring in and out.

A loud rumble from outside pulled my attention away, getting quieter in the distance. Through a sliver of vision, I saw the truck reversing, having taken much less damage than our frail vehicle. Then it stopped. It was going to ram us again.

CHAPTER 4

My body ached. The crash looked much worse than it sounded. I got up and brushed the dirt off my smooth leather jacket, only to fall to one knee. The horse was unharmed, but the wheel had snapped off causing the carriage to drop several feet. It appeared I had been launched out into the uneven cobblestone street. Horse—wait, *what the hell was going on?*

"Hey there! Are you alright?" A tight grip under my shoulder pulled me upright.

A tall blue figure lumbered into view. The brass buttons on his tunic reflected the sun, making me squint at first. No older than thirty with a full bushy brown beard, his peachy-toned face scrunched with concern. The silly hat gave me the impression I was watching an old BBC program.

"I said are you alright?" the man repeated, laced with a British accent. His striking blue eyes stirred comfort within me, despite the aggressive version of help.

I spit out what I hoped wasn't a tooth and rolled my head in a circular motion. Nothing broken, at least from the neck up. "I think so. Where am I?" I managed in a hoarse tone. My accent sounded a bit more proper than the stranger's, more of the common British I had heard in other places.

"You must have taken quite the hit to your head. You're in Whitechapel. I hope your memory comes back soon. I've been waiting for you for weeks."

My focus returned, giving a clear view of the area. Two and three story Victorian style buildings lined both sides of the rocky street. Pedestrians milled about without care on the ample sidewalk space. A few of them watched with looks of concern despite offering no help. I made note of their dress—dark and muted browns, tans, and grays. Long overcoats on the men, draped dresses for the women.

A horse-drawn carriage passed by, the rider shouting an obscenity at having to dodge the mess in the street. After I settled my stance, the stranger in blue let go of his grip and walked over to the horse.

"She'll be okay. I'll have someone bring her to your quarters," he said while detaching the harness. "We've arranged a room above a local pub during your stay."

I rubbed my hands over my head and face—short hair and a smooth chin, a sensation I hadn't felt in years. From the look of my clothes, I was somewhat out of place. Dark blue trousers—pants, why did I call them trousers? My newly scuffed up black leather overcoat was thick and appeared expensive, underneath a muted blue suit coat, and... badge. I turned it upward to read it upside-down.

"Yeah, that's you, Inspector," the stranger laughed. "I suppose you don't remember our correspondence yet, but all in good time. I once took a wallop from a mugger and forgot my morning!" He extended his hand for a shake.

"Constable Timothy Green. I wish our meeting was more pleasant. Let's get to work."

AFTER DROPPING my belongings in the room, the constable led me to his local office. As we walked into the superintendent's office, a sickly déjà vu crept over me. Had I been here before? This was my first time in Whitechapel, but it looked so familiar. That was seldom a good sign. A strange series of thoughts broke through an invisible barrier before they fluttered out the window with the smokey air. *Was I in a coma after the car crash, or was I dreaming?* I had experienced vivid, often lucid dreams enough times, but they were never easy to discern from true memories—if there was a difference in my case. The thoughts snapped away, back to Green waiting for me to step inside.

The cramped office had enough room for a few bookcases, with more knick-knacks than books, two chairs, and a desk, placed in front of the small window. A brawny, well-dressed man overlooked the busy Whitechapel street, a hand on his hip. Green closed the door behind, jostling the man out of his thoughts who turned to face us. While dressed similarly to Green, the blond man's uniform was tailored to fit his frame and darker, matching his sun-kissed face. Even his stance was proper, accenting the brightly polished buttons and highlighting the lack of a crease in his clothing.

"Green." The man nodded and leaned into his chair, the uniform bunching up to show his muscles pressing against it. "So, this is our savior?" A thick layer of sarcasm coated his words.

"Superintendent Williams, please meet Inspector John Hales from the Kensington district, City of London Police."

Hales. The name rang a bell, a dull one. I approached the desk to greet the hesitant superintendent. To my surprise he took my hand, albeit tightly, and motioned to sit while he adjusted back into his chair.

The non-existent lumbar support reminded me of a backache I didn't know I had, causing a jolt of pain.

Thwap.

A newspaper connected with the sturdy oak desk, shocking me out of my thoughts and causing me to flinch. I hoped nobody had noticed.

"A mite jumpy are we?" Williams said with a snide smirk, the sharp features on his face accentuated. "Kensington is known more for their museums than their murders, Hales. I don't know how much help you'll be to us here."

I held the newspaper and glanced over the headline— *The Whitechapel Murders: Two More Victims.* Hand drawn black and white depictions of grisly murders scattered the first page of the earthy, almost rotten smelling paper.

"I apologize, superintendent," Green said while looking at his feet. "Hales took a nasty spill into town. He's still regaining his faculties,"

"Well, I hope you have your wits about you," Williams said. "We've been trying to make heads and tails of this so-called *Butcher.* But to be honest, if it wasn't my job, *and* in my backyard, I wouldn't give a damn."

I set the paper back on the desk and looked over to Green, uneasy in his seat. "What the superintendent means is that—"

Williams cut him off. "What I mean is that these *women* shouldn't be wandering the streets at all hours of the night." His words were laced with barbed wire, cutting through any sense of decency in the small office. "If I haven't made it clear, it's the commissioner that wants you here. My men are tired from interviewing drunkards and fools. Do what's necessary to stop this. And keep out of our affairs."

"WHAT WAS THAT ABOUT?" I said, as we ambled out into the street.

"Stuck in his way. And gets in all of ours as well," Green said, shaking his head. "He doesn't speak for the majority here. He claims to hate women, although he's seen with a new one every other week. And he's bitter. I went behind his back and called on the commissioner to get you here."

More thoughts flowed through my brain. The headline and conversation must have jogged the memories loose. I'd been part of the police force. Initially a constable, I was promoted to inspector soon after for years of good service. I'd weeded out corruption back home in Kensington, mostly peers taking bribes to turn a blind eye. The higher ups saw potential in me—this was my big break. So far, four women had been found horribly murdered and the local police were stumped. London was panicking.

"So," I said. "Let's get started."

CHAPTER 5

Darkness fell over the city, a thick blanket of fog settling over the downtown square. The lamplighters had just finished illuminating the streets, the smell of sulfur lingering in the air. It had been a few weeks, and with each passing day, Williams grew more overtly annoyed with my presence. After a not-so-quick mailing, my superior calmed him, but the tension was palpable at every meeting.

After several more days of investigations—interviews, stakeouts, late night patrols—I began to side with Williams. Why was I here? Making no progress and yet another body, the pressure continued to escalate. This time mutilated and disemboweled in even more gruesome fashion. I could still taste the vomit on my breath despite the vigorous salt and charcoal scrub. As I chewed on peppermint leaves hoping to ease the feeling, I spread the case files from each murder on the oak desk in the room I had been calling home.

I ran my fingers across a now stubbly chin. Shaving was low on the priority list these days. Searching without direction had been fruitless. I needed a plan. "They're all women", I said out loud leaning back in the chair. *Not much to go on, Sherlock.*

So far, the investigation only yielded that the women were from the lower end of society. Prostitutes, servants, laborers. The public got wind of it, and from those I'd interviewed, the women of Whitechapel feared for their lives. Even most streetwalkers were staying home or took extra precautions, many forgoing their work as long as they could.

He—I hated to stereotype, but I just knew it was a He —somehow got close, breaking their every safety provision to inflict unspeakable horror. Maybe he's charming or rich? Handsome or a smooth talker? Or he knows them. No, too many women from different backgrounds for that to make sense. I'll wager he's using a position of power or authority to lure them. Someone they can trust. I needed to think in terms of the postman, perhaps even clergy or a public figure of some sort. Or a doctor.

He has some knowledge of the body, focusing on organs—albeit crudely. The murders looked quick, but he spent time with most. Undisturbed too, probably occurring after sundown or early morning. And he must have had easy access to any location without looking out of place. Easy entrance and exits, blending in with the world around him. Able-bodied. The women may have been small, but they were jostled about, several appearing positioned intentionally in public.

And what would make a man do this? Maybe scorned by love, but more likely a break from reality. My gut said he's no young buck. Twenties, early thirties, I'd wager— although this type of evil doesn't stay hidden for long. It's not often someone suddenly loses their marbles. Ha—*I'm even using the lingo now.*

I opened the desk drawer and pulled out a notepad

and my new fountain pen, a gift from my old partner in Kensington. Scribbling onto the heavy wood pulp, I let the black ink flow. *Male. Healthy. Trustworthy. Blends in. Positions of Money and or Power. Aged 20-30. Night owl.* I paused for a beat, then continued. *Takes pleasure?* It wasn't a great start, but it was something.

The urgency grew with each day. And the killer showed no signs of stopping. He had to slip up soon enough. It was time to get back on the street.

IT WAS NOW WELL past the witching hour and Whitechapel was fast asleep. Except for her. The light emerald gown flowed in the slight breeze. Much under-dressed for the crisp autumn night and no older than twenty-five, she carried herself like she had seen the world ten times over, peering over a shoulder at every block. Her long blonde hair, tied together with a tight pink bow, matched the extra rosiness on her face.

She darted across an intersection, avoiding a puddle of horse droppings that the night soil men had yet to collect. Her ankle landed on an uneven piece of stone, throwing off her balance to open the slit in her gown ever so slightly. The long, smooth, porcelain leg shined in the moonlight. A primal urge stirred within, a reminder that this amount of skin was not something I had been accustomed to, at least from a woman whose name I didn't know.

I regained composure and slithered back in the shadows. Where did she go? I just had eyes on her! Foolishly, I allowed lust to cloud my vision and lose the target. Target —poor choice of words given the context.

My eyes scanned the poorly lit street, landing on a dark alleyway between the druggist and tailor. Absent of fear, I did the exact opposite of any sane person— walking into the darkness after midnight. In an unknown area. With a serial madman on the loose. Green had taken to calling him The Ripper—the pseudonym from the letter in the papers. Most of the force doubted its authenticity, but the silly name seemed to stick.

The flickers from the street lamp illuminated just enough to see piles of trash accumulating on the sides of the yellow-hued brick buildings. The deeper I drifted into the alley, the darker and colder it became. Pinpricks of ice stabbed as heavy wisps of fog obscured my sight. I fought the urge to turn back as the anxiety finally kicked in, warning to end the pursuit.

"Dont fucking move," a woman whispered in my ear, coinciding with the cold, sharp blade on my throat.

CHAPTER 6

I swallowed hard, Adam's apple grazing the blade. My skin felt icy at first. A thin bead of liquid danced down my neck until it kissed my collar. The faint smell of iron proved she was serious and showed her knife was extra sharp. My bravado, or stupidity, was on full display standing frozen in the darkness.

"You even twitch and I'll slice you open," she said, confidence and vitriol in her voice.

I paced my breathing, the blade still tight on my throat. The Butcher, a woman? Was my theory wrong? The victims were all women, but that meant nothing right now.

She pushed even harder, more blood trickling out. Small but forceful fingers ran over my body, exploring and pinching my sides. A surge of pain shot through from a sharp pressure in my hip. My Webley revolver. I'd been carrying it around for days, but suddenly the memory of how to use it emerged.

With a quick pull from my overcoat and a loud clunk on the cobblestone, the pistol was now a dozen feet away, clouded in darkness. "A gun?" she said with a deep apprehension.

I hesitated to speak, the blade dangerously close, but mustered a few words. "Why are you—"

She didn't give me a chance to finish, interrupting as she continued rifling through my pockets, my coat gradually feeling lighter. "What's this?"

The pressure ever so slightly eased while I envisioned her reading my badge. "A... bobby?"

Her hand tore from my neck. As she stepped back, boots clacked against the stone, echoing through the empty corridor. I turned to face her, cautious in every movement, just in case she had any last minute reservations.

"I thought you were..."

"The Butcher?" I finished.

Her eyes narrowed, studying my face. I was busy doing the same. That beautiful face. Her bright green eyes glowed in the dark alley, accented more by the color of her dress. My gaze drifted down, drinking in her curves.

"See something you like, inspector?" Her tone, a blend of annoyance and mischief.

"I, well—" I grabbed at my neck, wiping a small trace of blood before clearing my throat. "You shouldn't be out here. There's a killer on the loose."

She settled onto one leg and placed a hand on her hip. Her lips curled into a devious smile, tapping the knife against her thigh in an exaggerated motion. "From the look of it, I should be giving you the pointers." An eyebrow raised as she cocked her head, giving enough pause for me to realize the stupidity of my warning.

I shook my head in embarrassment. "I mean, you can't trust anyone. Not even a badge."

She tilted her head, studying me even more intently, giving the impression she second guessed letting me free. A few more steps separated us, her backing closer to the street, the weapon slowly rising.

"That's not a threat, miss..." My statement, disguised as a question, lingered in the air long enough to count my heartbeat a dozen times.

She relaxed her stance, the point of her knife still aimed at me from her hip. "Sophia. Sofie."

From her body language, it was clear the dump of adrenaline was wearing off, as was mine. Her eyes darted and settled back on me, her instincts intact. She was no butcher, but I had no doubts she would follow through if she needed to—her presence was just as sharp as her blade.

My protective nature took over, questioning her actions—out so late alone. Her eyes rolled toward the top of her skull. I realized I became another overbearing man telling her what to do. Accepting my apology, she explained her friend was murdered nearby while searching for work. Surely a fellow prostitute. After a few barbs about the law not helping, she took matters into her own hands—prowling the streets, hoping to run into the killer.

"You're playing a dangerous game, Sophia."

"Sofie. And what do you care? All I hear is talk and all I see is death. The way I see it, I have a better chance of finding him than you."

Bloody hell. She was right. I had narrowed down the list, but the chances of catching him in such a wide net were slim to none. Green and his men were on board, but with most of the force following Williams' lead, Whitechapel was too large for us to cover. And if my theory was correct, I couldn't trust many.

I paused, struggling to find the right words. "Maybe we can work together?"

CHAPTER 7

The high pitched whine faded. "Can you hear me?" The voice slurred, echoing in my eardrums. I faced the noise, squinting to make something out of the blocky colors around me.

"There! He's movin', I told you he was alive!" the voice said, this time with less reverb, more coherent.

A powerful hand jostled me forward.

"Don't move him!" another voice screamed. "He's covered in blood! You're not supposed to move them!"

The voices gradually gained clarity, more distinction between the two. The world remained a brilliant display of lights. And I was cold. So, so cold.

"Are you a doctor?" the older voice said.

"No, they always say that on the TV shows. Did you see what happened?"

"A black truck t-boned 'em outta nowhere, blew the red."

The lights tightened, more focus—I was upside down, struggling to follow the conversation.

"He's coming to!" the younger one said. "Don't move buddy, I called the cops, they're on the way. You're gonna be OK." He looked toward the other voice. "What happened to the driver?"

"It was nuts," the old man said, now with more grit. "Two guys jumped out of the truck, took—"

I cut him off with the loudest, most guttural inhalation I'd ever experienced, propelling upright like a horror movie villain back to life. My vision was clearer, air was crisper, and a new fire flowed throughout. I looked down to see the bloodied clothes. Running fingers over my forehead, the wetness had already started to dry.

"Woah!" both men exclaimed, jumping back in shock. I couldn't blame them, any sane person would have done the same.

I sent a hand under the blood soaked shirt. Smooth, unbroken skin—not a scratch. Quinton once mentioned injuries caused by Tempus members were non-fatal, healing supernaturally fast. This was the most intense experience I had with it, apart from witnessing others.

I craned my neck toward the wreck. The car lay totaled, flipped over, and appeared to have gone through a meat grinder. And here I was, getting to my feet like I had taken a light tumble.

The men stood frozen with jaws dropped. I shook my limbs, then cracked my fingers and neck. My left arm felt funny—tingly and numb. I attempted to roll my shoulders, but only the right side listened, the left uncooperative. The reflection in the scuffed car paint explained the sensation: my left shoulder was rounded and abnormally protruded. Without giving a second thought, I grabbed the limp wrist, threading it under a knee. While balancing on one foot, I pulled the numb arm using my knee as leverage until hearing the loud pop. The arm instantly regained sensation, pins and burning throughout.

"Woah! Calm down dude, we can get you to a hospital. They can make sure you're alright!" The young man seemed more alert than his older counterpart, whose face was flush, appearing on the verge of sickness.

I didn't have time for a hospital, especially with the clock ticking before the day reset. A siren in the distance stole our attention. Instinctively, I used the distraction and sprinted away from the scene without looking back. My feet pounded on the cement, unbalanced at first, drowning out the yells from the good samaritans. Now over a quarter mile away, I slowed to catch my breath, walking alongside a dense treeline guarded by an old chain-link fence.

A small tear in the fence proved wide enough to snake through. A scattering of droplets fell from the sky as thick grey clouds drifted close. I positioned myself behind a large ponderosa pine, then glanced back through the chainlink barrier. An ambulance parked near the scene, with a police car rolling up seconds away. The two onlookers stood near the one-car wreckage, speaking to a paramedic. The younger one pantomimed explosions. His hands shook wildly in the air while the older man stood in disbelief.

Who hit us, and where did they take Vance? I had to let Lotus know. The cellphone! I searched my pockets. A sigh of relief—it hadn't fallen out. I hovered my finger on the screen, ready to tap. Shattered. Just my luck. A loud slam boomed from the distance.

A generic matte-black sedan had parked next to the ambulance. The dangerously pale man in his fifties leaned against his door, waiting with cigarette already in hand. The driver hopped out next. The twenty-something woman's reddish-orange hair was even shorter than her partners, spiked into a frizzy, fashionable look. She set a neon colored tumbler on top of the car while she buttoned her jacket, garnering an eye roll from the man.

I studied their body language, their cheap suits, trying to figure them out while the young black woman took lead and walked over to the group. The conversation appeared one sided—everyone but the pair talking after the initial greetings. The pale man approached the young onlooker, who remained relatively still. After a minute of chatter, the young man pointed directly in my direction. Like in a comedy, all six heads turned.

I sank low into the foliage hoping I wasn't spotted. With the fence, trees, and at least a half kilometer between us, I might have been safe. But with that many eyes, I couldn't take any chances. They would head here soon either way. I poked up to see the two suits sauntering closer. The woman was on a cellphone while her partner chatted the police close behind. At least they weren't running. I figured I should be.

As I RAN through the forest, careful not to leave too much of a trail behind, I took stock of the last few hours. After the last year, especially thanks to the dwindling echoes of my life in China, I had just got comfortable, easing into a seemingly everyday, run of the mill life. Now thrust into a secret mission, getting rammed by a psychopath, and now running from some people in suits—it felt familiar. A little *too* familiar.

"How can the same shit happen to the same guy

twice?" I muttered under my breath, borrowing a line from John McClane after he too realized danger seemed to follow him.

I kept a steady pace through the dirt, mindful not to twist an ankle on the slick, uneven soil. Those suits didn't seem like they were from Orchid, or any part of Tempus I'd seen. But how did they get here so fast? They must have been tailing me or whoever hit us. Quinton said he had eyes on me. Maybe they were on my side? I decided to follow my instinct and keep moving. With Vance missing and presumably captured, if the old samaritan was to be trusted, I was dealing with a brand new threat. I could figure out who was after me later. First, I needed to get in touch with Quinton or Melissa. While... *that pull.*

My heart fluttered. Electrical pulses fired into the lymph nodes near my neck. An arrhythmia, I heard Dr. Carter say from within. I had been watching too much TV while I waited for my next order this year.

She was close. I could feel her. The sensation was deep. Familiar, but different from the one at the diner. If I believed in auras—and as a time traveling reincarnate, there's not much I don't believe in—I imagined this being a different hue of one I'd been around before. I didn't dare speak her name and get my hopes up.

Orchid, and their stronger trackers like Vance, were drawn to other travelers over long distances. But from what Quinton explained last year, some special bonds transcend any role or ability. Someone important was nearby.

A twig snapped from behind, breaking me from the trance and severing the connection. I scanned the surrounding forest. Stillness. Giant old trees over twenty feet tall towered over me. The hard rain had turned to a light drizzle, giving my clothes a fighting chance to dry under the deep leafy coverage. The after-rain smell gave a sense of calm, a stark contrast to my current heart rate. I took a moment to pause and leaned against a tree, dropping my shoulders to ease the tension.

"Freeze!" a woman's voice boomed from the distance.

CHAPTER 8

If there's a running theme so far, it's that I let my guard down too easily. Especially to women, apparently.

"I got him, sending coords now," she said, the chirp of her walkie punctuating the sentence.

How did I miss her? Initially obscured by some loose bushes, she eased into plain sight. Her grip on the pistol tightened, trained on my chest. She looked even younger up close, maybe just a few years older than me. A thin cut ran down her cheek, more pronounced by a clenched jaw, her teeth gritted tightly together. The dark suit was now covered by a black waterproof jacket, a few strands of orange hair poking out from a black beanie.

The sensation inside flickered again before burning out like a candle. Somehow I deciphered the feelings, interpreting the somatic into a silent understanding. The woman I was sent to find *had found me*.

We stood in silence for what felt like an hour. The back of the tree became comfortable, leaning on it fully for support. In the distance, lightning cracked over her shoulder followed by heavy rain. She didn't flinch or even blink as far as I could tell. It was surreal, staring at each other, studying each other. I tried to read her mind, using body language and facial expressions. Anger? No, deeper —revenge. I didn't know who she thought I was, but she wanted me dead.

Heavy droplets fell around us, the rain breaking through the treetops pouring in. It took me too long to realize she was waiting for backup. Try to dodge a bullet or get caught? I'd learned Tempus bullets couldn't kill me, but hers? Either option not good, but from her expression, I didn't have much time to decide. Her twitchy finger seemed to have a mind of its own, *although she hadn't pulled the trigger.*

Another loud crack of thunder, this time much closer. Her eye twitched, giving me the first break I'd seen in the stone gaze. I took my chance.

Twisting my torso behind the tree in one swift move, I sprinted away using the giant oak as my shield. I hoped the rain obscured her vision more than it hurt my escape. With wide footfalls, I bounded through the wet, rocky ground, intentionally pushing off the balls of my feet to open my stride. I stretched out my arms, forgoing stealth to keep my balance—almost losing it more than once. That changed after two bullets whizzed by.

The loud ringing jolted my focus, causing me to lose balance. I tripped and fell hard into a fallen tree, the crunch of my neck even louder than the next bullets that flew by. I crawled behind the log for cover as another bullet exploded close, chunks of wood splintering into the air. I checked my body. A quick scan of limbs and extremities—she missed, for now.

"He's on the move," she said from a distance. "You want to die like this?" her voice bellowed from behind. From the volume, I gauged her at least fifty feet away.

I spotted a drop-off on the ground beside me and quickly used it to crawl undetected from the shooter. Another round cracked through the forest, shattering the log I had just used as a shield. She was blind in the dark, rainy forest. But I was trapped. Another two shots in rapid succession, one splashing water from a puddle into my eyes.

"Mara!" a gruff voice yelled from her direction. "Are you trying to kill him?" he said in a hushed but forceful tone, loud enough to hear. I slowed my escape to listen in.

"Get your hands off me!" she said. "He's one of them! You're letting him get away."

More branches snapped as water splashed. They were either on the move or struggling with each other. Even if the man wanted me alive, I couldn't take any chances. I lifted myself up and sprinted down the decline, fighting gravity the entire way.

"There!" she shouted.

I ignored my pursuers and focused on my next strides. Run first, think later. The sound of rushing water grew, a pleasant change from bullets. As I darted through the trees, fighting uneven wet terrain and gravity, my survival instincts amplified. Adrenaline coursed through-out, helping to dodge the tiny pools and branches with quick, fine movements at a second's notice. My body gave no signs of stopping, my heart and lungs working in tandem to power through the elements, even increasing my pace. My mind was sharper, eyes clear, calculating the best direction to take instinctively. Until the cliff, that is.

The drop was steep, almost a ninety-degree angle. I came close to falling over, having to send my weight backwards not to crash into the icy river below. From first glance, the drop looked at least a hundred feet. Jagged rocky shards and thick tree roots lined the descent before opening up to a medium-sized pool flowing into a river. Nearby, a small waterfall fed brownish-gold water down below. No luck gauging the depth, the fog and rain obscured anything giving me good measure. I was at a dead end and the suits were coming in close.

Another choose your own adventure—get captured or jump? I wasn't invulnerable, but surviving a car crash made me feel I was. Tempus can't kill me, but I had never tested a self-inflicted injury. Could I survive myself? *I've seen this work in the movies.*

"Stop right there!" the man shouted close by. "And hold your fire!"

I glanced over my shoulder. The pale man stood a dozen feet away, pistol drawn. As I turned back to the water, a rustle from behind him drew my attention. The woman sprinted out of the bushes, directly at me. And she wasn't stopping.

Here goes nothing. I pushed my toes against the soil, springing forward to avoid the edge. The descent was fast and cold. My insides jumbled, ears popping from the rapid pressure change. The exhilarating freedom, untethered by earth, until the crash of pain danced through my nerves. I expected a loud noise but only found silence. Until the sinking cold wrapped me in a pressured cocoon of darkness.

CHAPTER 9

I brushed the water off my face with a washrag, eyes still weary from the night.

"That's the last of my things," Sofie said, slamming a heavy bag of clothes on the floor.

We decided it best to stay together during the next few days of our experiment, especially with her work slowing from The Butcher. Her finances took a hit. And the protector in me had worried every time we parted after our meandering nights in the city. I hated the idea of using her as bait, but she proved she could take care of herself and was smarter than I gave her credit for. I could profile the killer all I wanted, but luring him out had a much better chance.

She looked around the small room, her emerald eyes stopping on the single bed pushed against the wall, turning into a squint. "We certainly didn't think this through, did we?" She brushed a strand of hair out of her face and gently shook her head with a coy smile.

"I'm used to sleeping on the floor. We'll make do," I said casually, not acknowledging she was right. We made the decision quickly, but coordinating our nightly trips had become a burden.

Her well-groomed eyebrows raised. "We've been

working together for over a week, and I hardly even know you."

"Not much to know, I suppose. I feel like there's a question in there for me."

"I understand it's your job, but why do you care so much? About this case?"

"Stopping murders isn't a good enough reason?" I said with open palms, taken aback by the question.

"To be honest, yeah," she sighed. "I suppose I see the worst in people. Neglect, abuse, people just thrown away. Even by the law. Sometimes, *especially* by the law."

I nodded. "I see it too." I walked over to the desk and pulled out a chair to face her, sitting on my bed. "I try to be the difference. Maybe I'm naïve. But you're right, when I came here, the man in charge wasn't too happy. It was almost like he wanted the murders to keep happening." A chortle escaped my mouth.

She leaned forward and bit her lip. Our eyes locked in silence for a moment, both likely thinking the same thing.

AGAINST MY URGING, Sofie left to visit a friend, hoping to learn more from the word on the street. I hoped the bright sunny afternoon would deter any killers. Plus she was only a block away. That didn't stop the churning in the pit of my stomach. She had grown on me—her crass-ness, her quirks, the resilience of everything she had been through that got her here.

The knock on the door took me by surprise, although I figured Green would follow up at some point. We'd been checking in every other day with little to no updates, to both of our frustrations. I opened the flimsy wood door. Green stood with an uneasy smile, avoiding eye contact—a stark difference from his usual optimistic self.

"Come on in." I extended an arm for a warm welcome.

He ambled in, his clasped hands pressed tightly against his nose and mouth.

"You look as though you've seen a ghost," I said, closing the door then walking to the tiny stove. "Some tea?"

He broke from his gaze, eyelids fluttering then scanned the room. "No, I—you have company?"

Sofie's bags were scattered on the floor and bed. I hadn't clued him into our plan. Even with the trust I felt with Green, things had seemed off since I had arrived in Whitechapel. A gnawing sensation not strong enough to pursue.

I shifted back in the chair. "It's a bit of a story. I've recruited someone to help me. Help us. The less you know, the better." I set my mug on the desk, now fully focused. "Is something wrong?"

He watched the steam rising from the cup as he spoke. "When you first arrived—" He stopped, closing his eyes until looking back with an intensity. "Did anything feel... *strange* to you?"

Wrinkles formed across my forehead. I studied his body and tone. Things *did feel odd* when I arrived. And in this moment that only amplified. The edges of reality began to crack while a lucidity fought to break into this dream, this memory, whatever *this* was. I now realized as the days and weeks had gone by, I was watching events unfold. Not fully in control of what was happening, merely reliving the past, minute by minute. I broke away momentarily, wondering where my body was. *I remembered water.*

His voice echoed, audible yet murky. "By your response, or lack of it, I can tell I've frightened you," he said, more confidence in his voice.

Focus returned to the room, drowning out the thoughts of another world, pun intended. "It's not that. But yes. Things seem a bit *different*. But if anything, I've felt I can trust you. From the moment we first met."

"I'll come out with it then. When you arrived, the broken carriage." He waited a moment for my nod. "That wasn't the first time we met."

I took a sip of tea, much too hot for my liking. Some spilled on my pants as I briskly pulled it away from my mouth.

A brief smile crossed his lips before returning to the serious expression. "You arrived a day earlier. No broken carriage. We had dinner, met with Williams." He paused, rapping his fingers together with a grimace. "It didn't end well."

"I don't follow." I leaned back propping a foot on my knee. "End?"

"It defies rational thought, but I sense deep inside you know it's true. After dinner, a mugger attacked us. You didn't survive." He stopped to rub his hands together. "I didn't believe it when I first experienced it myself."

My trust wavered as it fought against his strange story. The absurdity was softened by my own apprehensions— the fleeting images of misplaced items and recurring events I had disregarded as travel-related nerves. "How—how is that possible?"

"You see, several years ago, I too lived my day again. I didn't understand initially. The realization came in the nights after. A waking nightmare of a robbery gone bad. Mortally bad." He inhaled deeply. "But in reality, I never entered that bank. Instead, I stopped the thief in the alleyway, no bullets fired."

A normal, sane person would have laughed him out the door. Or took this as a ruse. Something to lighten the mood of the gory horrors we'd seen firsthand over the weeks. A fantastical tale from one of the creative men touring the libraries in London and Paris. But no—he was right. Deep within I knew he was telling the truth. I nodded softly, puzzled but hanging on his words.

"Even after the dreams, I convinced myself it was hysteria. Nerves from the job and promotion. I put the events behind me until weeks later, a man approached me after a routine shift. He seemed to know about my nightmares. Not in detail, but the things he said were more direct than the typical con man." He looked at his feet, tapping his toes on the wood planks. "I felt ill at ease near him, yet intimately connected."

The more he spoke, the more things made sense. Blank spaces of time. Moments I couldn't account for. My own checkered history. I often got the sense the past was repressed, although that's not the word I would have used at the time.

He exhaled and the seriousness lifted briefly. "You haven't run, which is telling. When I was first told all this, I wanted to run but didn't either. Maybe the curiosity won out."

He was right again. I needed to know more. "The man, who is he?"

Green cleared his throat while the door opened. Sofie sauntered in with an elevated pep in her step. "You'll never believe—Oh, hello," she interrupted herself after seeing Green sitting on the bed.

He stood and nodded to her, extending his hand. "I apologize for intruding, ma'am. I was just leaving."

Just when he was getting to the good stuff. Sofie had terrible timing. I would have asked her to leave, but he said his goodbye and escaped before having the chance.

The abruptness did not go unnoticed. "What on earth was that about?"

CHAPTER 10 

Sofie was silent for a beat, twirling her long blonde locks while she rubbed her lower lip against her teeth. "Are you sure we can trust him?"

"Yeah," I said, with a slight tremble doing a poor job to convince her. "He's one of the good guys."

"Well, he sure as bloody hell went mad when he saw me." She leaned against the desk to take her shoes off, flinging one against the door with more force than necessary.

I dodged the second, playfully aimed at me. "Did you learn anything?"

She wiggled her shoulders, more agitation and excitement than when I saw her last. "I visited that friend I told you about. Boy, has the rumor mill been going!"

My eyes widened in waiting. She was building the suspense, making me wait before spilling the details. "And?"

She carefully scanned the tiny room, her eyes roving the shadows, wary of anyone possibly hiding or listening through a crack in the dusty floorboards.

"The past few weeks," she spoke softly, "there's been a drop in the regular patrols around

Hanbury Street. A few girls said before the murders, they'd see at least one bobby a night."

I nodded, following along.

"What is most peculiar," she continued, "after the second body, the patrols increased. Three, up to four peelers making the rounds. But then suddenly, nothing."

I scratched at my developing beard, growing some length after weeks of disregard. "That is odd. I get diverting attention to other areas, but completely scaling back in what may be the heart of the murders, that makes little sense."

She lowered her head and watched intently, her expression saying *"Obviously"*.

I shrugged with a hesitant smile. "Interesting. That gives us something though. You find anything else?"

"No. Everyone is scared. People are staying in as much as possible. Even the homeless are drifting further away."

I took a deep breath and exhaled. Eager we had our biggest lead in weeks, nervous that it brought us closer to danger. With her directly in the middle of it. "Let's say we check out Hanbury tonight?"

"Sure," she said, walking over to her bag. She pulled out a knife and set it down, making a loud clunk on the desk. "I'll be ready."

I HATED the idea but she didn't budge, giving me little say in the plan. We rented a room in the small inn across the street. The third-story window had an ample view showing her propped against the wall in the dark alley. My tea grew cold, over an hour going by well after midnight. She looked bored, occasionally pacing between buildings, blowing wisps of breath up into the cool autumn air. I was uncomfortable—not only fearing her being so far, but with how intently I was watching. She had a playful air about her. Even as a piece of meat in the jungle, she found some sort of joy prancing about.

Three men sauntered near. One slowed, seemingly muttering something crass before continuing onward. She waved him off and resumed pacing, finally settling on the other side of the wall.

In the short time watching, I counted a dozen pedestrians walking the street. The only law presence came from a bobby knocking his club on every sign and lamp post as he walked by. Was her contact wrong? Hanbury Street was quieter than usual, but it was nowhere near the emptiness we expected.

The hours ticked by, at times my mind drifted to the conversation with Green. Shortly after he left, I went by his office to hear he had taken a sudden departure. The secretary noted it was a common occurrence but wouldn't give any details. The timing was unnerving—my questions would have to wait.

I peered down at what I nicknamed Sofie's Landing. She was gone. My heart skipped a beat as I sprang from the chair. I leaned out the window, scanning the streets to see two men stumbling aimlessly. The other direction showed a couple on a casual stroll much further away. It was her! I rushed out of the room and leapt down the stairs, almost tripping over my feet on the uneven steps.

The chilly breeze tickled my face first, then shocked the rest of my body alive. I had left my coat and hat in the room, only equipped with a light cloth shirt and trousers.

Luckily I had been wearing boots, now pounding on the stone in her direction. They had quite a lead, but I didn't want to blow my cover either. I shifted into a quick jog, then a brisk walk, hoping not to draw any more attention. Now nearing four in the morning, several lamps had extinguished making the prowl easier.

I studied the man walking with her: tall, well dressed, young. He peered back, allowing a quick glance at his face. While familiar, my mind was a blank for names. Thankfully undetected, I swallowed hard and continued with caution. He fit the profile and we were in the thick of the killings. This had to be him.

She played her role to a T, hanging off his arm, exaggerated laughs, waking side by side. I replayed her words, hoping to put me at ease. *I'm going to lure him away. You keep watch.* Despite not hearing their conversation, the only fear I sensed was mine.

They took an abrupt turn, skipping into a dark alley, hand in her lace gloved hand. I hastened my pace, checking a pocket to find the pistol remained where I left it just seconds ago. At least I had remembered that. A bead of cold sweat dripped down my forehead, tracing an icy path to my eye. I brushed it away, running a hand through my hair then turned into the alley—just in time to hear the loud thud of a steel door.

Another loud clash, this time much closer. My wrist felt raw and wet, waves of pain then numbness flowed to my fingertips. My eyes opened, then closed instantly, shielding me from the bright lights drilling into my brain. A steady beep ticked away overhead at a soothing, rhythmic cadence.

"I'll get the doctor, he's up," a voice circled nearby.

I opened my eyes again giving them time to adjust. The bright white ceiling caused a hard squint, slowly gaining focus. Silver poles and gadgets hovered above wires descending to meet my body. Straining to see through the blur, fluid leaked down my cheeks. I tried to swallow, only tasting concrete. A blast of air suddenly tickled my nose. I wiggled my lips, grazing the plastic tube secured above.

One more loud crash, this time directly in my ear. I jumped forward only to find my wrists were bound to the frame of a bed.

"Yeah, you're not going anywhere," the voice said.

I craned my neck to see the suited man, arms folded with a smug expression on his pale face. He appeared older up close. Deep lines crossed his forehead while he studied my poor attempts to break free. I collapsed back onto the pillow, realizing I couldn't break the handcuffs.

An attempt to speak produced the faintest cough, followed by saliva dripping down my chin. Despite the pain radiating across my body, not being able to wipe myself off was even worse.

"Good morning Mr. Doe," a cheery woman walked into view. "Had quite the fall, have we?"

I nodded, or the room spun, nausea forcing my head firmly into the pillow.

"Okay, okay. Take it easy. I'm Dr. Shen." The forty-something woman adjusted a white coat covering the faded Nine Inch Nails t-shirt. A tight ponytail pulled her skin, overly emphasizing the pair of bleary brown eyes. "I'm going to take the oxygen out. We'll give you some-thing for the dizziness." She leaned forward and gently unwrapped the tubes from my face.

The man flanked my other side, bumping into the bed. "Be careful, he's dangerous!"

"The cuffs gave that away, officer," she said dryly, shooting him a look of annoyance.

"Special Agent, *thank you.* I need to have a word with him now. Alone."

Their short exchange was tense. What the hell happened here and how long was I out?

"Suit yourself, *Special Agent.* He might not be too talk-ative." She wiped the fluid from my eyes with a piece of gauze and backed away. "A few broken bones, hypother-mia, lacerations across most of his body, not to mention a possible air embolism we're monitoring."

"I'll take my chances. Thanks doc."

The door closed behind her, leaving me with the

older man. After draping the suit coat over the bed, he rolled the sleeves of his wrinkled dress shirt. I spotted a faint black tattoo, military perhaps, etched into a hairy forearm. "I'll give you a chance to do this the easy way. Just say the word."

My lips pursed. Even without hearing a question, I wasn't in the mood to talk.

"Your call." He briefly disappeared, soon returning into view tapping a small tube. "You got about thirty minutes before my partner gets here. If you think any of this is bad, well, she was ready to shoot you dead." Overhead, I heard the rustling of plastic as he manipulated the IV.

Within seconds, heat coursed through my body, swirling from my chest to my crotch, stopping at my toes. The sickly taste of rotting garlic filled my mouth. Dizziness. Then a memory flashed by. Hands clawing at the icy water fighting to climb through the depths. The woman, his partner, jumping into the water. A sharp pain in my temple. Some sort of fight in the river. Had she knocked me out?

He cocked his head, one eyebrow raised. "Yeah, you remember something huh?" He shook his head and blew air from his nose.

I opened my mouth but only coughed again. The third attempt, words finally came out. "Wh- Who are you?"

"What's more important is who are *you?* And who was the man with you?"

"Vance?" The word blurted out without thought, breaking through any inhibition.

A loud rumble of laughter bounced in my skull as he

clapped his hands together, thunder in my ears. "Yeah! This stuff always works. Tell me everything."

A pulsing fluttered in my neck, heart rate increasing, fighting a dull calm within. I wanted to yank at the handcuffs, but felt too weak. And weaker. *Weaker.*

"I juussst met him.... today. He'sss kinda a dick." There was no controlling the words. They flowed out like the coffee my captor casually sipped.

"Okay." The man nodded, pleased. He faded into a blur then melted back into focus. "Who does he work for?"

"He's part of—" My larynx snapped shut, a painful tightening within causing me to gag.

The man stumbled backward, dropping his mug while he grabbed his ears. He continued flailing, knocking over a tray of medical supplies until his back was against the wall. Violently shaking his head, wide eyed, he braced against a chair before standing upright. A machine beeping above increased in speed.

I must have been smiling. "You think that's funny?" He slammed a fist on the bed rail. "You might be our only lead and he got away! Who hit you?"

The door burst open. Dr. Shen stormed in followed by a security guard and nurse sporting looks of concern and shock.

"His vitals are skyrocketing! What the hell did you do?" the doctor said, checking a machine to my right.

"I need answers!" the agent shouted.

The brutish security guard stepped between him and the doctor. The beeps grew louder, faster, my vision blurred into a fuzzy mess. Noises blended together making it difficult to hear.

"Check this out," the nurse said, holding up a vial to the doctor.

"What the fuck! Sodium thiopental? Are you trying to kill him?" the doctor screamed at the suit. "Ted! Get him out of here!"

The guard drew a pistol on the agent, who raised his hands and backed out of the room. "I'm a federal agent! You can't—"

Shen didn't let him finish. "Get him the fuck out outta here!" She turned to the nurse while rustling around me. "We need lytes! Charcoal! Shit, he's fading! Get a crash cart in here!"

More noise and voices filled the room. "Tube him!"

A loud boom, then air washed over my skin. The sound of rumbling from every direction. One eye peeked open showing the ceiling tiles running away in the opposite direction. Voices blended together into one solid, warbly mess of noise.

CHAPTER 12

I hated that I was getting used to this feeling—waking up from a haze, either medically induced or otherwise. Rubbing alcohol and iron crossed my nose causing me to flinch then recoil away. With the way today was going, I could only guess what I would see when I opened my eyes. A soft beeping grew louder, followed by the rest of the clatter soon after.

"He's coming to," a voice bounced around my head. "Let Shen know, she wanted an update."

My eyes twitched, breaking open through layers of crust. I was thirsty. My throat burned with a dryness I hadn't felt—a lifetime ago. A man in bright blue scrubs towered above.

"Hey there, I'm Nurse Hulett," he said. Even younger than me, he boasted a neatly shaved baby face. "How are you feeling right now? In any pain?"

The words felt foreign at first. "Well," I paused, taking stock of the room. Bright, sterile. I wiggled my toes and fingers then shifted around in the firm bed rolling my neck. "I feel like a hundred bucks."

"Good, good, uhh." He flipped through a clipboard almost dropping it, obviously not finding the botched colloquialism funny. "You were in pretty nasty shape. Do you remember what happened?"

"I remember—"

The door shot open, startling both of us.

Dr. Shen sauntered in wearing dark blue scrubs, mask hanging under her youthful, tired smile. She yanked off her gloves and surgical cap while approaching. "Thanks nurse, I'll take it from here."

The nurse nodded and retreated away after picking up the papers he had fumbled.

Shen grabbed the chart and sucked air through her teeth, eyes glaring at me with a smirk I couldn't place. "Well, Mr. Doe," she said now seated, setting the chart on my lap and rolling over on a stool. "I've got good news, bad news, and weird news. What'll it be?"

I focused on her face, the expression showing a playful confusion along with... a trace of concern? "I could use some good news." My throat hurt. A memory of someone telling me to cough before a tube left my throat caused a shiver.

"Alright, good news is you're alive." Some cheeriness left her tone. "The bad news is we're getting heavy pressure from the feds to discharge you into their custody."

"The feds?"

"The ones who brought you here." She motioned to the bedrail. "Hence the handcuffs. A prisoner?"

"News to me. I don't know what's going on."

They must have knocked me out good after that dive. Clearly my plan to wash away safely backfired.

"Yeah, I figured. I put the pieces together pretty quick, but their credentials check out."

A thirst burned inside causing another cough. I

searched the room, landing on the styrofoam cup far out of reach. Reading my mind, Shen grabbed it and placed the straw to my lips. After a long pull of ice filled water, I ran my tongue over cracked lips, savoring the brief relief. "Is that the weird news?"

"No." She set the cup on the nightstand. "Weird news is your broken bones aren't broken anymore. Your cuts and bruises have healed, and your vitals look perfect. I'd say you're in tip-top shape. I did find, however," she paused, reaching in her coat pocket to pull out a small clear plastic bag containing a reflective object. "This."

I squinted, trying to make out the device no bigger than a USB drive. In fact, I was almost certain it *was* a USB drive, and much smaller than the ones available in the stores right now.

She set the bag on the nightstand. "It was a few layers under the skin, above that peculiar barcode tattoo. Which has changed colors a few times while you've been here, I might add."

Shit. I did my best to ignore that thing. Especially since it hadn't come to play in the last year. It changed colors based on Tempus' presence—specifically if I was being tracked, from what I remembered. Why didn't Vance mention it earlier? I looked up at her, waiting for me to reply.

"Uhh..." I was at a loss for words. How could I explain any of this? The nausea didn't help.

"Yeah. Now seeing your reaction, I figured your *magic* healing and all wouldn't be a surprise." She stood from the stool, arms crossed with a stern expression. "Your turn. What the hell is going on here? I've been stalling them, but I can't fudge your vitals for much longer."

I appreciated her openness, but I had a bad habit of getting too many people involved. The last time I asked for help, I almost put a pawnshop owner and his friend in the middle of a fistfight. "The less you know, the better. Why are you covering for me?"

"I see a lot of patients. Some in handcuffs. There's something different about you. When you first came in your—" she stopped, staring so deeply she might as well be an ophthalmologist. "Eyes," she whispered, full of curiosity.

I've leaned on these baby blues before. Not that I thought I was the most charismatic, even when I was a grammy winning rapper in an alternate future. But when I looked intently, with purpose, people seemed to lower their defenses. I tried not to abuse it. But coming in unconscious—what did she see?

The doctor snapped out of the daydream. "And I hate to stereotype, but I've never heard a clearly European guy speak more fluent Mandarin than me, at least around here." She paused and blinked rapidly before continuing. "Although your dialect seems *somewhat dated.*"

My lips curled into a faint smile. "I'm actually a little rusty. My Japanese is better."

What had I said? In the early years, my dual racial identities caused plenty of issues from the internal conflict. I eventually leaned into it, trying to combine the two in a way. By using the stage name Hagaki, I shared a remnant of the past, albeit to an unknowing public. Of course, that too came with its own conflict.

Dr. Shen crossed her arms again, forehead turning into wrinkles then shaking her head. "At one point you were singing a song," she lowered her voice and leaned onto the railing. "My great-grandmother would sing it to me as a baby. At least that's what my mother told me."

The bed lightly shook while a faint buzz radiated from the doctor. She pulled away and craned her neck downward. "Damn, they're paging me again. These people really want you." She leaned under the bed for a few seconds, returning into view after a loud click. "I'm not sure this is the right thing to do." She paused to look behind, finding we were still alone. "But what you do next is on you."

She tapped a button on the monitor above, winked, then turned and walked out. I was alone with the silent machines *and* one bedrail unlocked. With just enough room to push forward, I slid the cuff down and off the rail. One down, one to go. Using my free hand—well, as free as it could be with a loose handcuff dangling—I pulled out the IV and disconnected the chest leads.

Now I just needed to free the other hand. I twisted over the railing to land softly on the floor. With my shackled arm contorted, the other hand searched under the bed blindly until finding the button unlocking the railing. Freedom! I made a mental note to send the doc a Thank You note—If I made it out of here before the suits came back.

CHAPTER 13

Lucky for me, no guards were posted at my door. I popped my head into the dark hallway to find it surprisingly empty. It appeared they had hidden me away in a seldomly used wing. I ignored flashbacks of the late night horror movies and took stock of the floor. A single nurse sat at the end of the hall, busy clicking around on their screen.

Handcuffs dangling off each wrist wouldn't make for an easy escape. First order of business, find something to break free. I crouched, then duck-walked down the hall, keeping low to stay out of view. After a safe distance, I stood and searched the surrounding rooms.

Each hospital room was unoccupied, with neatly made beds waiting in the darkness. Tissues, furniture, TV—all stocked with the same general items and none that could help pick a lock. I snuck from room to empty room, hoping for anything to free me. Finding something to cut through the steel seemed even more unlikely. And while I might easily heal, dousing my hands with chemicals sounded painful—if I could even find something powerful enough to melt steel.

I sauntered into another room, wondering if my hands would regrow after cutting them off. The old man gave me a shock at first. The still, silent old man, deep in a coma. If the hospital had a floor to hide patients away, this must be it. I shook my head and laughed, wishing he could appreciate the situation.

After fumbling at the locks with a pair of surgical scissors for far too long, I calculated my chances of just running out the hospital, deciding I wouldn't get very far. Now back in the hallway, I noticed a new, less dangerous solution. I pushed open the door marked "Linens" and rifled through the drawers until I found a set of scrubs that fit. Long sleeve ones. I doubled back to the old man's room and used half a roll of surgical tape, securing the cuffs to each forearm then covering them with the sleeves.

Now dressed to blend in, aside from weird bulky arms, I *borrowed* a surgical cap and mask from a nearby cart and headed the other direction toward the elevators. A nurse materialized out of a doorway, trotting in my direction—and to my room.

"Prisoner is all set for a while," I blurted out, mumbling through my mask while giving a cheesy thumbs up.

She stopped and scratched her head.

"Orthopedics," I said, continuing with the power walk. "You can check back in about thirty. Don't waste your time."

The nurse shrugged and turned around, disappearing back into the room. Sometimes you get lucky, I guess. Blind confidence and pretending like you belong doesn't hurt either.

I froze in front of the high-tech display showing the

next elevator heading to my floor—a maybe not so lucky number seven. Damn, that must be them.

Not wanting to take any chances, I darted through the stairwell door and sprinted down the stairs until reaching the lobby floor. I pushed the ER door open and fought for air through the mask. Shen leaned on a desk close by the overzealous suited man I had the displeasure of meeting earlier. From her face, and the badge he was waving inches from it, the conversation was not friendly.

I gave myself a moment for a deep inhale then grabbed a supply cart, wheeling it in their direction. My eyes began to water. What was that smell? I looked down and realized my scrubs were clearly not from the clean pile, radiating a stench of iodine, musky cologne, and body odor, causing me to gag. If anyone caught a whiff, maybe it would cause them to scurry away.

As the cart inched closer, I listened in on their conversation.

Grateful for whatever effect I had on the good doctor, Shen remained committed to helping. "Your partner is already on her way up there to get him," she said, rubbing one of her bloodshot eyes with force. "Badge or not, it's after visiting hours and we have a one visitor pol—"

The suit interrupted, doing a poor job of keeping his voice down and lacing the words with ire. "I just told you. Whoever's up there *is not* with me. My partner is on her way here right now. Where did you move him?"

Another visitor? No time to worry about that right now.

A short stocky man rushed through the hall, narrowly dodging a tiny frail woman gripping her IV pole. After apologizing, he used the frayed necktie to wipe beads of sweat off his forehead, exposing armpit stains on the wrinkled dress shirt. "Shen, I'll handle this. Special Agent Blake, I just spoke to your office and I'm truly sorry for this headache. I assure you we—"

"Get to it," Blake interrupted the man. "Take me to him. Where is he?"

I stopped the cart a few feet after I passed, crouching while pretending to look through the medical supplies.

"Yes, of course. Room 788. He's at the..." the administrator trailed off, watching Blake turn and storm toward the elevators.

The agent flipped his cell phone open and attacked the buttons, tapping his foot impatiently for the next lift. A stupid, risky, but possibly enlightening idea crossed my mind. *This might be my only chance to find out what's going on.* I spun the cart toward the elevator door, which was just about to close. Blake scoffed after the door sensor triggered, letting me roll on in, just the two of us. Hoping my stench, disguise, and his preoccupation on the phone would be enough distraction, I sank to the back corner after calling for the eight floor.

Blake nestled the phone close, whispering. "Hey. He's on the seventh floor, room 788,"

I resumed my role pretending to take inventory, acting as unassuming as possible. The other end was too quiet. I'd have to make do with one side.

After a few floors, the agent's head drifted in my direction. I leaned away, reaching for a bag obviously out of grasp on the far side of the cart. In the shiny door's reflection, I caught his nostrils flare before he jolted his face away. The stinky clothes helped after all.

"What's the status on the other team? Are they still tailing the truck?" he said after an exaggerated cough.

Passing floor five. I'd only have a few more seconds of information, but I'd take what I could get.

"The desert? I wonder why they are headed there." Floor six. "Ok. I'm almost to his floor. I'll wait for you before I go in. Let's get our information and dump him, then rendezvous with the other team."

Floor seven. The door opened and I stayed put.

I waited as the door closed while he sauntered away and finished the conversation. "A minor setback. Not sure what this has to do with Lucian, but they definitely targeted thi..."

Wait, what. Lucian?

CHAPTER 14

I stood motionless, staring out from the elevator into the eighth floor. A nurse hurried by snapping me to reality. I hit the lobby and door close buttons in rapid succession before leaning on the railing.

Did he say Lucian? Former leader of Orchid, behind the plan to kill me-Lucian? It was too much of a coincidence to be anyone else. But last I saw him, the mysterious robed leader of Tempus dubbed "One" had frozen Lucian into a statue next to Alycia, the Lotus traitor. Come to think of it, Quinton mentioned he hadn't heard from One in months, which he thought *unusual.*

The elevator dinged and stopped on the second floor, opening for two doctors. With a nod and warm smile behind the mask, I recalibrated and focused on getting out before solving any mysteries. An intense wave of energy washed over, starting at the base of my neck and flowing into my toes. *The woman from the forest was near.* Could she feel the same thing?

The doors opened into the lobby. I motioned for the doctors to head out first, wheeling the cart after them. Through the partially open blinds, Dr. Shen and the portly admin were locked in a heated discussion, the muffled barbs muted by the break room walls. I saw her glance in my direction, although I doubted she could tell it was me. What else I had told her in my twilight sleep?

"Nurse? Nurse?" I realized the elderly man was talking to me, pleading from the waiting room.

"Uh, I'll be with you in just a moment, sir," I lied.

Before returning to the cart, the corner of my view locked on to Blake's partner. Walking stiffly with chest out, she appeared ready to pounce. Her head twitched toward me then returned forward with laser-like determination. If Shen *was* telling the truth, who was the visitor she mentioned earlier?

The warm sensation flowed, this time stronger—paradoxically making me weaker. I braced the cart against the wall, channeling the strength of my upper body to ride through the wave. My legs soon regained sensation, now seconds from the ER entrance. My chin swiveled involuntarily, forced to look over my shoulder to see the spikey haired agent waiting for the elevator. She shook her head, holding it with one hand like I often did when a headache struck. The coast was clear. I ditched the cart and walked out the revolving emergency door.

The cool, fresh after-rain air tickled my skin. Freedom once again. The sun was nowhere to be found in the gloom of the morning clouds. I took a final peek through the foggy ER windows, catching the woman press a button as the elevator doors closed. Her eyes widened in my direction, then shrank into a squint. Shit.

I turned and fell into a brisk pace heading toward the parking garage. Had she spotted me? Hopefully, she wrote it off and headed to her partner to find my empty room. I broke into a faster pace, throwing off the mask to help my airflow.

No money, no keys, no phone. I had to contact Quinton somehow and figure out what the hell was going on. I suppose I could steal a car, but I hoped I didn't have to go down that road again. Running it is—again. At least until I figure this out.

"Hey!" a woman screamed from behind.

I launched into a sprint without looking back.

"You can't run from us Jay!" the shouting bellowed further away.

At least she wasn't shooting. Yet.

The loud splashes echoing behind announced the chase had begun. The head start helped as dizziness swirled around me, pushing massive amounts of air through my lungs with each giant stride. I glanced back to see her struggling with her phone, still a safe distance away. I'd have company soon.

I darted up the broken cement stairs leading into the garage, stopping on the third floor. The smell of oil and exhaust creeped past, trailing an old two-seater with a rattling muffler. The floor was almost full, giving a full range of vehicles to hide behind.

"He's in the... parking garage," the woman huffed, reverberating several levels below from the stairwell.

I crouched alongside a pickup truck double parked, blocking a fire lane. Hopefully she didn't see what level I ran to, giving a few minutes to catch my breath and form some sort of plan. Despite the clean bill of health, my body fought the waves of heat and pressure pushing into my temples. Stealing a car sounded much more alluring right about now.

"You can't hide forever!" she shouted, much closer.

Damn. She was on the same floor. I went prone and shuffled underneath a vehicle. Heat radiated from above—the car must have parked recently. I held my breath and listened. In the distance, water tapped in a rhythmic pattern sounding similar to the beat of my first hip-hop track. Tuning out the jam, I sunk low on the slick ground and remained still.

Despite her smaller frame, each meticulous footfall was heavy and seemed guided with precision. The rubber crunched against the dirt and debris on the concrete, my heart beating with each loud thump. The noise continued until the combat boots paused directly in front of me.

"I know you're close! I can..." she paused, continuing with contemplation in her voice, *"feel you."*

If only I could turn the tables and interrogate her and her partner—I had just as many questions, if not more. The boots tore away, crunching a few feet from my hiding spot. She sighed loudly, clearly frustrated.

"Look," her voice echoed off the cement walls. "It's obvious from the fall that you're a survivor. I'm putting my gun down as a sign of good faith."

Her long legs bent while she crouched, settling the gun directly into view. A few more inches and she would have caught me hugging the oil-stained ground under the truck.

"I just need answers," she continued in a more conversational tone. Her boots scraped on the ground, turning further.

While she was right—I could survive a hell of a fall and a gnarly car wreck—she underestimated the fatality of her bullets ripping through my head or heart. Bullets from a Tempus member? Sure no problem. From a regular human? Sayonara. At least it wasn't a theory I wanted to test right now.

With her back turned, I crawled forward and grabbed the weapon off the ground then retreated under the truck, rising from the other side. The sickly strange yet comforting sensations made me feel I could trust her, but I wasn't in a position to take any chances—I hated what I was about to do. Pointing the pistol half-heartedly from my hip, I crept from the shadows maintaining aim on her torso.

"I could use some answers, too." My voice came out gravely and with more confidence than how I held the gun.

Her about-face was instant. Shock and anger flashed across her face, eyes landing on the gun. She looked at me, no signs of fear while holding herself in place. With every second of silence that passed, I imagined she was sizing me up. Calculating how to end me with her bare hands.

"You know how to use that thing?" She smirked, condescending as expected.

Up close, I got the first good look at her. The smooth, dark skin from before was now littered with a smattering of small butterfly closure strips, dried blood crusted one of her ears. Without her hat, the spiky orange hair was even more of a mess, and a few inches longer than from afar.

I shot her a snide smile. "You're prettier without your gun."

She rolled her eyes and feigned a short laugh, not acknowledging the lethal weapon between us. "Still cocky as ever. How long have you been working with him?"

Still? I raised an eyebrow of my own. "How do you—you have to be more specific. Right now the only person I work for is me. In the shitty little dive bar I own, unless you count the manager I hired. Who are you?"

She folded her arms and bit her lip, looking deep in thought unsure of how to proceed before speaking. "*Agent* Mara Stanfield," she said, wavering on the word agent. She *did* look young for a federal cop. She unfolded her arms and put her hands on her hips, pushing out her chest more assertively. "Jay *Hagaki* Bialy. Rich uncle Quinton set you up in San Diego last year with a curious amount of money and property. A known associate of Lucian Blackwood. Wanted by Interpol in connection to several known terrorist organizations across the world. Any of that ring a bell?" No longer yelling, her voice had a familiar, smokey quality.

"The L is pronounced like a W, thank you. It's Polish." I chuckled before returning to her question. "Agent, huh? Some kind of spy?" I asked, careful not to confirm any of the connections while fixed on her voice. Where had I heard it before today?

She smiled, watching me struggle to connect the dots. "I guess you could say so. You didn't answer the question."

"No, I don't know any Lucians. And not much about my uncle either, other than he's loaded and wanted to help after my folks died." Some of that was true—although both unrelated. I had left Detroit after my parents died. And Quinton had offered to help—or had been ordered to.

"He's caused a lot of pain. That's not good enough, Jay." She punctuated my name with the same anger in the forest. "No coincidence he crashes into you and takes your hostage. But why leave you?"

Hostage? Vance. She must think I'm part of a terrorist cell. What did the government know about Tempus? We were supposed to be an ultra secret organization. "Is that why you're trying to kill me?" I started to lower the gun until I saw her eyeing it and adjust her stance, readying to attack.

"I was aiming for your legs," she said with another chuckle. She could have fooled me.

I watched her eyes intently, her gaze slightly changing as a quiet thrumming approached from the distance. Shit. She has been stalling again. I made the mistake of looking toward the noise, catching her lunge from my periphery. I stepped aside and turned, leaping over the hood of a sedan, then sprinted between the rows of cars with her close behind. The bright lights from a helicopter beamed into the openings of the garage, aimlessly searching while I carefully used the vehicles to provide cover.

While racing toward the staircase, I pulled back on the pistol slide and popped it from the bottom, tossing it behind and ditching the other half under a car. It wouldn't do me any good—I wasn't ready to add to the death toll—but they sure as hell wouldn't return the favor. The helicopter was nearing the garage walls, drowning out the sound of sirens growing closer. Now I was really out of options.

Skipping the last five steps in favor of a leap, the jump brought me seconds away from Mara's footsteps clashing behind. They joined the symphony of boots closing in from every direction.

"Give it up, we've got you Jay!" Mara yelled from the stairwell.

I turned for only a moment, a near fatal mistake. Burning rubber accompanied the high-pitched squeal as a silver sports car glided from the darkness. The expensive vehicle drifted its rear, grazing my hip with a soft tap to stop precisely at my side. The driver's tinted window lowered, revealing the last person I expected.

"Get in," Alycia ordered.

CHAPTER 15

Another loud crash. And then silence. I paced back and forth outside the heavy, worn door. Nothing audible crept through, even after pressing an ear to the metal. The panic intensified. Questions flooded my brain. How long do I wait? Why did she go in here? Did she have a choice? They were laughing it up just a moment ago, all according to plan. We never clarified *when* I should act, other than a call for help if needed.

A soft thud escaped from the door, the first noise since hearing it shut. Time was running out, each second adding a sharper pressure in my chest. After a minute of nagging fear, I decided to take action. I pulled hard at the handle, receiving only a short groan for the effort. It shifted ever so slightly giving a flicker of hope, but I needed a new approach and fast. I rocked inward and outward, finding a rhythm in the dark alleyway. The door was durable, but the frame had a few too many years of disrepair. The lock eventually snapped with a puff of acrid dust and tumbled onto my foot. I kicked it away and opened the door with ease, illuminating the alley in a yellow glow.

The dull office was scarcely larger than the room I

had called home the past few weeks. And empty. Papers lay scattered over the desks, sure signs of a hasty exit after a day's work. Near the furthest wall, a long staircase led up to a single green door, *Manager* scribbled in faded paint.

A faint, high-pitched yelp. Was I too late? I bounded the steps forsaking a silent entry in place of speed. With momentum on my side, I smashed a shoulder into the door, breaking through as shards of wood scattered in the air. The splintered door swung back and slowed before falling off its hinges and smashing on the wood floor.

"How dare you!" a gruff voice shouted from the corner. "What is the meaning of this?"

The only light came through the windows. The faintest sunrise mixed with the remaining gas lamps outside cast an amber hue on Sofie, perched atop a desk like a stage actress awaiting her spotlight. Head arched down, her glowing hair cascaded over her chest, exposing a soft pink neck. From the shadows above, trembling fingers pressed into her shoulder. Sofie looked up and smirked, messy hair flowing about.

"Are you okay?" I gasped, still out of breath.

"Do you know this man?" her assailant asked, removing his chubby digits to wiggle them at me.

"I guess the law says we can't have any fun, Danny." Her mischievous smile grew bigger.

"WHAT ON EARTH WERE YOU THINKING?" I said, pacing our small apartment room.

"It was almost daytime, and it was obvious nobody

was coming tonight. I wanted to have some fun," Sofie said, untying her boots then throwing them into the corner. She exhaled and pressed her back on the small sofa I had been sleeping on the past week—I offered up the bed, the gentleman I was.

"Well, this isn't the time to have fun," I said. "I'm on the job. I was a fool to think you wouldn't be too."

She stood abruptly, jabbing a sharp finger in my direction, face red with enough heat to warm the room. "What's *that* supposed to imply?" she said, practically lunging with her words.

"I mean to say, it's not even safe to pick up one of your customers. Even if we're turning up with nothing." My tone was parental, condescending. I cringed internally, but the damage was done.

She belted an exaggerated laugh, shaking her head.

What was that response? I scrambled to backtrack my judgments. "I—sorry. It's a living. I get it. I understand I've been footing the bill here, I know. If it's about money, well, don't worry. You don't have to work right now. We're a team." It was work. Not something the lawman in me was fond of, but work nonetheless. But was my anger truly about her profession?

"Are you aware..." She loosened her posture, running fingers through the loose blonde strands and tucking them behind an ear. "You've never even once asked what I do. I'm not a whore, not that it is any of your business. I'm friends with some. And was friends with more, until The Butcher."

My heart sank. First the embarrassment, now fully realizing the relationship was based on assumptions.

Then came the anger—at myself for not having an actual conversation and getting to know her.

I swallowed hard. "I uh... the other man?"

"An old flame. I knew you'd come, eventually. I told him you might. But if not, who knows?" A faint but genuine smile crossed her lips.

Another swirl of emotions. The anger quelled, turning to relief. Then morphing into—was I jealous of that man?

I stood and approached her. Without saying a word, I peered deep into her eyes. She relaxed even more, appearing surprised, dropping any sign of the vicious fighter from before.

"I was afraid of losing you," I said

Her touch sent a shiver down my spine as her hand gently rested on my hip. I let the green eyes bore into mine, melting away any fear or doubt, if only for a few moments.

CHAPTER 16

My lips bathed in fire. Burning pulses shot through every synapse, flooding with an ethereal ecstasy that no organic or synthetic drug could match. Something I knew a little about from my early celebrity life. The sensation abruptly turned to pain and then nothing at all. Moonlight beamed through the windshield to cast a soft glow on the leather glove torn from my face.

"Good, you back in reality?" said a proper British voice.

I turned to Alycia while massaging the feeling back into my lips. "Huh?"

"You were unlocking. That's the quickest way to snap out of it." She raised a knee to secure the steering wheel while sliding her naked hand back into the glove. After dropping the knee, she placed a hand back on the wheel. Her other hand shifted to a higher gear, aggressively jolting the car. The engine cried and erupted with more power. I fought a cough from the heavy fumes, oil and gasoline mixed with rubber. "All I could find was a manual. I've been spoiled with autos the last decade."

Dazed, my gaze drifted up to the moonroof. Lights flashed by with milliseconds between. From the speedometer, we had reached over eighty miles per hour, still gaining speed. She danced through the minimal traffic with ease, almost as effortlessly as Quinton the last time I was rescued. I sure played the damsel in distress well. Thankfully, it appeared we were on the freeway, although the tinted windows made it difficult to spot much detail. Just as I settled into the cushion, a rhythmic chopping erupted from the sky.

The helicopter lowered into view, eliciting a "hmph" from Alycia and a heavier foot on the gas. The shaky chopper fought the elements, eventually stabilizing and kicking on an ultra bright spotlight. Nowhere near our vehicle at first, the light zig-zagged the road, soon sending its blinding rays through the glass. A palm shielded my eyes from the burning as Alycia tore at the wheel, veering across several lanes to dodge the beam.

"Again, who is after you?" she snapped, head focused on the road ahead calculating each swift dodge between the lanes.

She was a stark contrast to the Alycia I remembered. Pre-statue, that is. A few long strands of blonde hair draped out of the black baseball cap, worn uncharacteristically backwards. The prim and proper makeup was replaced by a scattering of oil smears on her chin and forehead, matching the greasy, baggy blue overalls. I couldn't tell if the machine shop stench was coming from her or the supercharged sports car, but with these soiled scrubs I held back any comment.

I swayed my body to look behind. In the far distance, several white lights blinked, huddled together and following with a matching pace. The absence of sirens was eery, only hearing our engine and the aircraft in the sky.

"They want your *friend* Lucian." I added the emphasis —the least I could do to show I hadn't forgotten her turning on Lotus—and trying to kill me last year.

"*Who* are they?" She tore at the wheel again, dodging another beam of light. I squinted but soon found myself tossed to the side despite wearing the belt tightly. My head smacked the window with a soft thud.

I grabbed a handful of hair and groaned softly. "Ugh. I don't know. Government. They think I'm with Lucian and his terrorist organization."

She chuckled, darting past a semi truck that slowed to the parade of lights we led from behind. "Terrorist, huh? Someone hasn't been doing their job," she laughed again.

"What do you—"

She cut the wheel harder than before. The force caused me to gasp for breath mid-sentence. I pushed the entirety of my torso against the center console, protecting my head from snapping. The car zipped off an exit, no signs of slowing from the freeway speed. Alycia hit a button on the dash causing a small LED screen to drop over the radio. "Hold on."

We launched off the exit ramp, drifting ninety degrees onto a main road better than Vin Diesel. Her arm pulled the gear shift, again ramping up to excessive speeds. "Shut up for now, I've got to lose them." A finger tapped at the screen until an address popped on the display—three minutes away. "Good, it should still be there."

The car weaved through intersections, avoiding other vehicles and the bright helicopter spotlight. Most of the pursuers remained on the freeway, only two chasing at a safe distance. We drew closer and closer to the deepest parts of the city. Burnt out streetlights and abandoned buildings replaced the brightly lit billboards and busy storefronts we passed minutes ago. "Okay," she said, finally cracking a faint smile. "When we stop, get out and follow me. Understand?"

I nodded, not sure if she saw. Her eyes seemed locked on the derelict four-story warehouse ahead. The complex appeared abandoned for years. The only sources of light came from headlights and the helicopter darting above. In a swift set of motions, she shifted through the lower gears, soon slowing us to a crawl. A loud metallic grinding screamed from underneath. The focused woman let out a soft laugh, amused at her timing. If we had slowed just seconds later, the bumpy, pothole-filled road would have chewed the car's low suspension.

"Brace," she said, not giving more than a second to prepare as the car revved then exploded through the loose chain-link fence. The gate swung into a tiny security hut that clearly hadn't seen a soul in years. She tapped her finger a few more times on the console and a small loading bay door rose at the far end of the building. "Glad it still works, too."

"What is this?" I said quietly, doing little to hide the awe in my eyes.

"Questions later, get ready."

Without warning, the helicopter descended into view, hovering a few feet off the rocky parking lot. "We have you surrounded. Come out of your vehicle with your hands up!" a voice boomed from the speaker. I scanned the area—white lights sparkled from every direction, closing in on the gated campus grounds. Alycia swerved around the aircraft gracefully, resuming her path to the open garage door.

"This doesn't look good.." I said. There was no reason to trust the woman and from all appearances, she had let us into a deadend.

"I said shut up, just get ready."

The car eased into the small opening. With another tap on the console, the door closed behind as dim yellowish lights flickered from the ceiling. The lights soon stabilized to reveal we were in a giant, open concrete box. Well, warehouse, at one point. Glass from the broken second and third-story windows littered the smooth concrete floor crinkling under our tires. Through the faint light, I spotted a staircase on a far wall leading up to what must have been a manager's office. We rolled in that direction, stopping feet away from the stairs.

Alycia's door sprang open, her body a blur headed straight for the staircase. "C'mon!"

I hopped out and hurried after her, already halfway up the staircase. After only two steps, a blinding bright light encased the ground exposing the crystalized coating of shimmering glass. A second helicopter must have joined its partner, creating the beautiful, deadly sharp light show.

"Keep moving!" she said, tapping into the keypad next to the office door. I raced up the steps as the door clicked open revealing the small, empty beige office. A wood desk sat under a giant glassless window overlooking the factory floor. Goosebumps rose on my skin, staring out into the vast empty sea of glass. *This place felt so familiar.*

Remnants of the broken window crackled underneath, redirecting my focus to Alycia. She stood at a small door opposite the entrance. Another keypad—one I hadn't noticed earlier—beeped with each press until a loud click sent the door into the ceiling. And what was behind it? Of course: an elevator.

"Coming?" she said, while her face read *"let's go, you idiot."*

CHAPTER 17

We stood chest to chest separated only by a whisper of air. Our eyes darted in every direction, not finding anything to land on in the tiny, cramped, windowless box as it descended fast enough for my ears to pressurize. After swaying uncomfortably, our eyes finally met just before the lift groaned and shifted. Momentarily losing balance, we brushed against each other only to retreat back in the limited space. The baseball cap fell, sending blonde strands of messy, shoulder length hair flowing. Some stuck to the oil on her cheeks, partially obscuring her emerald eyes.

We studied each other in silence, staring, probably wondering what the other was thinking. At least I knew I was curious. I stuck my tongue out then laughed, hoping to break the tension. The faintest, and I mean faintest flicker of a smile crossed her face before the serious-as-stone demeanor returned. The elevator slammed hard, shaking the car sending us into the walls then each other again. We looked down to find my hands tight on her hips, which I immediately released, throwing palms up to my chest.

"Ooops," I smiled, still finding levity in the breakneck chase we had—or still might be in.

The door opened, Alycia grazing my side as she squirmed out first without saying a word. I peered into the darkness, only a tiny green light in the distance giving some concept of a destination.

"C'mon, dammit," she groaned, crashing noises coming from her direction until her flashlight cast a bright blue beam into the small hallway. A familiar woodsy smell flowed through the air, reminiscent of the station I visited earlier. In fact, the hallway looked remarkably the same, even though we were hours away.

I followed her tightly, passing a few closed doors while we walked toward the green light. "What is this?"

"Safe house."

We approached the source of the green glow, a small room lined with technology from the seventies, maybe early eighties. She dropped onto a stool, propping her elbows on the counter where three dusty screens sat. Her fingers mashed on the keyboard until the room lit, faintly, and green text soon sprawled across the screens.

She tapped a sequence on her smartwatch and stood from the stool to face me. "We've got three minutes until the factory above is toast. Five until everything underneath is ash." She turned and walked to the wall in front of the screens, running fingers across the smooth unassuming wall until nodding to herself. Without warning, she barreled her shoulder into it with enough force causing a loud crunch. She either broke a bone or part of the wall.

"Help me out here!" she ordered, giving the impression I should have been helping already.

I tripped over myself on the way, dumbfounded as she continued to ram the wall—now showing significant cracks spidering from the attack. "Let me try." I grabbed a monitor, a thick, heavy old CRT, and rammed it against the wall. On the third attempt, the wall gave way, sending me tumbling face forward. Pieces of drywall scattered while dust joined the air, glimmering in the beams of light from above.

"Up," she said, pointing to the source.

I cocked my head upward to see the tiny, secret room housed a rusty iron ladder ascending at least a hundred feet.

"I almost forgot," Alycia snapped, handing a black backpack covered in the white drywall dust. "Now we go up. Hurry along now." She slipped her arms through a backpack of her own and tapped the watch.

I touched the first rung, instantly recoiling my fingers from the frigid steel. Alycia cleared her throat then pointed to the watch. I brushed off her annoyance and turned to the ladder. Using the promise of burning in a fiery inferno as a motivator, I swallowed hard, grabbed the bar tight and grimaced with each pull upward. My fingers eventually grew accustomed to the cold—just in time for the temperature in the small, cramped shaft to begin to rise the higher we climbed.

"Brace yourself for the first one!" she yelled from below. "In seconds."

A golden haze illuminated the bottom of the shaft. The pungent odor of gasoline and laundry detergent ascended as the glow cascaded through the unmarked aluminum walls at a rapid speed. I fed my arms through the rungs, hooking them tight while shifting my torso to secure my legs on the bar beneath.

"Hold your—" She was cut off but I got the message,

palming my nose and mouth then squinting to avoid the brilliant yet blinding mirror show shining off the steel sheets.

A low rattle came next. Like the sound of a rattlesnake fading in. The noise intensified, sounds of a fireworks show punctuated by metallic warbles and popping of the aluminum siding in the escape shaft. The walls shook, thundering from below and rippling upward until passing overhead. The ladder suddenly plummeted, only a foot, but enough for my armpit to dig deeply in the rung. I bent backwards and screamed out in pain, grabbing my shoulder instinctively. Without time to readjust, the ladder shot back up to its original position, my sweaty fingers slipping off only to rely on my legs wrapped around the metal. Another loud crash, this time my doing, as my back and head smashed against the aluminum. Thankfully, the shaft was so cramped it held me upright after I lost my grip. I pressed a palm against the surprisingly cold, flimsy sheet, then grabbed hold of the ladder.

"That should be it," Alycia said, tapping on my shoe. "Keep moving before the second blast!"

There's more? Great. I followed the order and continued the climb. The air gradually changed from cold and musty to warmer and... more humid. A steady splashing echoed from overhead, albeit faintly. I glanced up to find that we had reached the ceiling. A dim light shone through a small clear porthole window.

"Turn over the lever," Alycia ordered. I giggled at the way she said *lever* like in the British shows I'd been watching and... living, now that I think of it.

I firmly gripped the lever and pulled, then pushed

out, swinging the ceiling-door open like a secret tree-house entrance. I pulled myself out and held out a hand for Alycia, who took my help before jumping back like I had some kind of disease.

We were now in a tiny room, if you could call it that. The brown, earth lined walls were bathed in a yellowish glow, swaying from the construction lamp as it dangled on the wood beam above. The uneven floor and walls were made of tightly packed dirt and stone, held into place by splintering 2x4s. A small archway led out to a dark corridor, sporadically lit by more lamps daisy-chained together by extension cables.

Alycia glanced at her wrist again and sucked air through her teeth. "Ninety seconds." She took off her backpack to pull out a flashlight. "Here." She handed me her bag and lit the corridor while pulling a cellphone from her pocket. "Shit." Her head bounced between the forks in the maze then settled on the center corridor.

Close behind, I maintained pace as she burst into a quick jog.

She stopped to mutter something at her phone before racing again through the underground labyrinth. "Bloody tunnels were much more organized in 2012." She shook her head. Even from behind, I imagined the look of annoyance. "There should be another ladder. There!"

She pointed to the frayed rope swaying above then attacked, pulling her muscular frame quickly—clearly climbing was part of her usual workout. My attempt wasn't as graceful, now fumbling for her hand in the darkness after reaching the top. Her grip tightened, helping to launch me into almost complete darkness to land next to her on the creaky floorboards.

I shifted my weight, readying to stand when I was pulled sharply to the floor. "Stay down!" she screamed.

More fireworks. This time closer and much louder, booming underneath. The explosions lasted seconds, followed by the world shifting as the earth groaned in horror from the assault. Having experienced only one earthquake, a five point something earlier this summer, this felt much more violent and personal. A thick dust escaped the hole we arrived through. Soon the room was filled with hazy, stinky air, triggering a series of hacking coughs. We scurried further to a corner with covered faces, while the ground rattled for another few seconds then settled, finally quieting.

"I think we're good," I said, finally standing with a wide stance in case I was wrong.

She spit out a glob of something into the shadows then clicked on a flashlight. The spotlight beamed around to reveal the foyer of a log cabin. A couch, bookcase, gas burning stove, and a stark lack of technology. I caught two smaller rooms in the spotlight, a bathroom and bedroom, both equal in simplicity. The light landed on a modest fireplace begging to be cleaned.

"Cozy place," I said, dusting off my shoulders and beard. "Where are we—"

The floorboards creaked and groaned even louder than before. A slight rumble slowly intensified—the earth decided it wasn't finished. A thunderous snap. Then the world tilted and melted away.

CHAPTER 18

I fell hard, only to be cradled by feathers wrapped tightly in smooth cotton sheets. A grey and white plume shot into the air, escaping from a small tear in the bedding.

"I knew you were a pushover," Sofie said before blowing a kiss from above.

I rolled over on the bed and pat the empty space in the linen.

She cocked her chin low and set a hand on her hip. "We can lay about later. I'm going to snap up that dress we saw in the shop. Maybe call on a friend, see what the word is out there."

"Back before sundown? He hasn't struck in days and I worry he's getting just as antsy as us."

"Of course." She bent down to plant a kiss on my lips. The taste of peppermint lingered after she pulled away. "Plus, I've got Marty with me." She tapped the hidden pocket of her coat, reminding me of the trusted knife named for her grandfather.

It was only three nights ago we shared a bed together, and since then, everything changed. I learned about her childhood, and in turn, I began to remember mine. It was as if talking with her jogged something loose in my soul.

My closest family had passed at an early age, tearing me away from native Scotland to live with an uncle in London. A police officer himself, I was often left alone for long stretches while he patrolled the streets in order to feed me, the unexpected expense he learned to love, even from afar. Bitterness fueled my sleepless nights, eventually leading me to follow his lead and enter the police force. I hoped to find redemption for what I lost, even though it was cholera that took my parents, not crime.

Rain pellets knocked on the window. The repetitive melody reminiscent of a beat I created during my bout with celebrity over a century and lifetime later. A memory still difficult to place, at least chronologically. With Green's partial revelation leaving me hanging, I found it all too easy to get lost in thought, now alone in the damp apartment room. Pieces of another soul broke through once more. The parallels of my lives pulled me deeper. Japan to China. Scotland to England. Poland to America. Every lifetime included a great voyage of sorts —to a fresh start in a distant land. Losing my family in hopes of finding a new one. I vacillated between comfort in the familiarity and the fear of being trapped in an endless loop, each pass a fresh coat of paint.

I lingered on the thought, wondering if there was a deeper meaning. With my three lifetimes of knowledge combined, I ran through every theory I could envision: Was this some kind of curse? My own personal hell, or a purgatory, stuck in limbo until I got it right? Or maybe a simulation like in a certain sci-fi movie. Except I couldn't slow time to dodge bullets, only arbitrarily jump backwards in it, pissing off anyone who noticed. The theories came from the novels and movies of my recent spin around the globe. Some more alluring than others—believing this was a punishment didn't seem too appealing.

A strong knock at the door broke me from the spiral, back to the warmth of my bedroom.

"Hales, are you there?" the man said from the other side.

I opened the door a crack. Green tipped his hat with a soft nod sending droplets to the floor. "Care for a walk?"

"In this rain?" I smiled, reaching for my overcoat.

Play it cool. A poor attempt to hide my eagerness—I rushed to bundle myself for the weather.

Green, with a hint of amusement, gestured to the hallway. "There's a quiet cafe down the block. We'll have more..." He paused, eyeing one of Sofie's bags on the floor. "Privacy."

"How do you know about this place?" I said, shaking my arms then running a hand through my rain soaked hair in the confined, dark vestibule.

Green ignored the question, opening the inner door leading to a hazy pub. From the outside, the unassuming paint chipped entrance was just another of the many found scattered throughout the dark alleyways of Whitechapel. The inside told a different story. A rush of tobacco flavored smoke forced me to squint through the tears. Deep mahogany walls set the tone for the aesthetic: dark, relaxing, and upscale. The patrons wore a variety of business suits or long flowing dresses, more elegant than what I'd become accustomed to. About a dozen sat scattered near sparkling rosewood tables, engaged in lively conversation with bubbling mugs or wine glasses in hand. Opposite the smoothly finished bartop, several onlookers crowded two men playing billiards—a close game from the look of it. How did they hide all of this?

"Those who aren't willing to look don't deserve to find," Green said, reading my mind.

Where had I heard that before?

Green looked back and shot a wink, then unbuttoned his jacket, shaking off the rain beads. I noted a new addition since we last met, a hand bandaged tightly with freshly tied gauze. Again gesturing to continue, I followed him to the bar, glancing around to take in the surroundings. None of the patrons looked familiar, despite me becoming a fixture in the area for the past several weeks.

Green approached the barkeep, a heavyset man with more hair than personality, pointing to a narrow ash-colored door at the furthest edge of the room. The bartender nodded, then nodded again after Green gave him the peace sign, which I soon realized was an order for two of something. Void of emotion, the hulking man turned and filled two heavy mugs.

I followed Green through the door down a set of exposed, uneven wooden stairs—the kind where someone can grab your ankles if they waited below. Through another door, this one requiring a key Green had tucked in his breast pocket, we walked into a smaller version of the upstairs. No billiards, bar, or other patrons —only a table fit for six at most. The decor remained the same, the heavy twinkle of sheen on the unbroken chairs appearing unused. This area didn't have many visitors.

"Hell of a place you have here, Green. I take it this is

yours? And on our salary?" I sank into a plush chair, making myself comfortable.

"A friend's," he said, a faint pinkish hue developing on his cheeks as he sat across from me. "I ordered us a meal, in case you were hungry."

"Whisky too, while you're at it. It's the least you could do to keep me waiting." I sat back smugly and cracked my knuckles.

"Let's stick to the D and B. Alcohol rarely plays nice with us, if you hadn't noticed."

His stone-serious face triggered a memory—strange, gin fueled visions swept through my mind. Rainbow mosaics melding into open spaces of purple flowery fields under a bright blue sun. My skin beaming with neon translucence. A comforting icy burn sweeping across my face and fully exposed skin.

Fingers snapped from a thousand miles away, and then again from across the table. "Yeah, thought so," he said, shaking his head with a grin. "Steer clear of the booze, I suppose that's your first lesson."

"Lesson?" I leaned forward, brow furrowed. "Enough of this horseshit, Green. We're supposed to be catching a murderer. What is the meaning of all of this? And why did you leave so suddenly?"

The door burst open. The barkeep lumbered to our table, delivering two plates of steaming chicken and vegetables. Our mugs sat atop each plate, splashing some liquid onto the food. So much for customer service. The giant caught my expression and grunted before storming off and slamming the door.

Green was overjoyed watching my annoyance at the spectacle. "Well," he said, pulling his plate forward.

"Have you told anything to the girl?" He took a swig from the mug, savoring the mystery beverage like this was a social call.

"Other than we're working to catch a killer." I took a moment to wrench at my beard. "We *are* trying to catch this sonofabitch, right?"

"Of course!" A dusting of crumbs spilled from his mouth. He chewed quickly and apologized. "I came straight back to you. I haven't eaten in a day."

"Then what is going on?" I toned down on the anger, just barely.

"Do you remember the man I spoke of? Before I left?"

I nodded and took a drink from the pewter mug. The earthy flavor, bitter yet comforting, hugged my tastebuds. A name trickled back. Dandelion and Burdock—this was my favorite.

"I was summoned to Paris. When he calls, I need to answer. *Especially* right now to avoid suspicion."

I circled a finger on the table, temporarily stalling the conversation before continuing. "The man you said you couldn't trust?"

"Yes. As I told you prior, I feel something around him, but it is an ungodly sensation. Not as with you." He winced in pain long enough to notice, holding his bandaged hand while taking measured breaths.

The days since our last conversation gave me plenty of time to stew and reflect on Green. When he was near, I felt safe. "What did he want?"

Green recounted his first meeting with the man. The secrecy and vagueness in their conversations. The uneasy feeling he had every time they met over the course of several years. How the man would arrive unannounced, or summon him across Europe to ask strange questions. Questions he finally could make sense of.

"This injury," he stopped, raising his wrapped hand. "This was my *initiation*. He is the leader of some sort of group. And he wanted to know if I had run into anyone such as myself." Green sat back after pushing away his empty plate. "It is now my..." He paused and shook his head, closing his eyes for a moment before continuing. "It is now my responsibility to report strange dealings occurring in London. In all of England. Strange dealings *with time perplexities*." He exhaled deeply.

"Perplexities?" I rubbed my hands together while adjusting to sit upright. "What—what did you tell him?"

"I said I would inform him the *next* time something strange happens." He smiled. "I was careful with my words so as not to deceive outright."

The gut feeling I had about Green was right. Protecting me from whoever, or whatever was out there. Tension left my muscles despite not knowing what I was even relieved from.

Green studied my reaction, head lowered while he wrung his hands. "Hales..." He looked deep into my eyes. "He was looking for you."

CHAPTER 19

Dust slowly settled, drifting through the light of the wavering candles. The blur of colors settled to reveal Alycia crouched on the uneven maple floorboards.

"Lucky. You almost fell back into the mines." With one hand cradling my neck and another wrapped under my arm, she wrenched me to my feet with one harsh pull. "Floor broke your fall."

I steadied myself after she released her hold. Looking to the ground I found she meant it literally—two of the wooden planks had shattered, leaving a crude impression of my ass surrounded by splinters.

"Thanks," I said, dusting off my clothes, soon realizing it didn't help with the oil and dirt stains.

"Here." She tossed over the backpack I held earlier. "Change of clothes. We're a few miles out and they should believe we're dead from the blast." She picked up her bag. "Let's try to keep it that way."

I unzipped the backpack and pulled out a pair of rolled up faded denim jeans. She had to be joking. The JNCO label stood out first. I held them out, watching the fabric comically unfurl for what seemed like a minute to reveal the giant, flared pants, each leg double the normal size. These were all the rage in the nineties, despite being highly impractical. I wondered how I got around without tripping over myself back in the day.

"Emergency kit hasn't been updated in some time," she said with a chuckle, holding a pink gossamer slip dress from her body like it was infected. "Clearly."

I shook my head and continued, finding a dull black sweater—plain, other than being a few sizes too big and about a foot too long. At least the chucks were timeless.

I scanned the cozy dark cabin for some privacy, eyes freezing on Alycia wasting no time changing. A flicker of candlelight reflected off her smooth tanned, naked back as she shimmied out of the oily jumpsuit exposing a cream racerback bra.

Before I could form a coherent thought, she glanced over her shoulder. Whether predicted or she felt my eyes burning from behind, she sent my gaze scurrying away. "Didn't fancy you a peeper."

Heat flushed over my face. If it wasn't red, it soon would be. "I'm sorry, I didn't—"

"Oh, I'm sure you're sorry," she responded with her signature confidence, not directly acknowledging my leer and even having some playfulness in her tone.

I spun around and peeled off the dirty scrubs, realizing I still had handcuffs taped to my forearms. With all the distractions, I eventually stopped noticing the uncomfortable steel pressed in my skin. Those would have to come off soon. I finished dressing, admiring the nineties skater getup. At least they didn't stink but I wondered if I'd draw more attention than intended. To my surprise, the shoes fit perfectly.

"You decent?" I said, facing away.

"Now you ask?" An exhale of annoyance from behind. "You can turn around."

I turned to see her transformation: a blue collar mechanic into a college girl ready to party like it was 1999. A white and black crop bomber jacket—complete with an S varsity letter—covered the glossy dress, medium black heels on the end of her muscular legs.

A goofy smile formed as I took in her outfit. "What's the S stand for?"

"*Bloody stupid*, like that smile of yours. You should see yourself." She adjusted a strap on one of the heels. "And how am I supposed to run in these fucking things?"

Still smiling, I pointed to my feet. The wide pant legs draped to the floor, each foot covered by denim. "Probably about as well as me."

Alycia rolled her eyes then scooped up her backpack, pulling out a tuft of platinum blonde hair. "Yuck. This'll have to do," she said, fixing her hair into the long flowy wig. "You should have a hat or hair in yours too."

I felt inside the bag, finding a snapback Detroit Tigers baseball cap. "Hey, they got something right." I put on the hat, backwards of course.

I pretended to adjust the outfit while secretly deep in thought. A year ago this woman tried to kill me. Now I'm awkwardly gawking at her while she adjusts a wig in a dusty old mirror. She had something special about her. Gorgeous, sure, but there was a certain charm that drew me in. Or maybe I was just lonely. I broke my gaze before being caught again. I didn't need any more guilt for watching, even though the first time wasn't intentional.

Something told me she wasn't a threat. Could I trust her? There wasn't much time to decide. I looked at my wrist. The watch was missing. Damn. Of course, hospital or feds must have taken it.

"Are you in a hurry?" she said, noticing me searching the room.

"Yeah, actually. What time is it?"

"Looking for this?" She smiled, raising her forearm, wrist donning a familiar watch.

"How did you—"

"I went up to your room but only found your belongings. From Quinton, I Imagine?" She flicked her wrist before dropping her arm. "It's almost noon, by the way."

My stomach sank. Less than six hours before the day would reset, if Quinton was right. Although, I had contact with the woman and nothing changed. Did I break the cycle? I decided not to take any chances. "I gotta get moving."

"Let's make it *we*, for now," she said, appearing satisfied with her new wavy hairdo and collecting the old clothes. "What's the rush? It might do some good to let the heat die down before heading out."

"I need to talk to Quinton. I've had no way to reach—wait, do you have a phone?"

With a break from the frantic chase allowing some clear thought, I realized Alycia might be able to reach Quinton, seeing as she was once part of Lotus, after all.

"I *had* one. Tossed it before I came looking for you."

"What! Why!" My anger surprised me, the frustration of the day had taken over.

"In case it was being tracked." She folded her arms defensively. "Not that it would have done you any good anyhow."

She was hesitant at first, eventually giving in to my

persistence. Her story sure sounded plausible but I listened carefully for any contradictions. She recounted the last year, frozen in a torpor, occasionally regaining a flicker of consciousness despite having no physical control of her body. Standing upright for months, she was stowed away in a crypt deep beneath the Tempus council chamber. Her voice trembled, pausing multiple times to close her eyes and compose herself. If she was faking it, she was a damn fine actor—it looked painful to recall the memories.

Unable to fight the urge, I gave in to the empathy tugging at my heart, hoping letting my guard down *yet again* wouldn't bite me in the ass today. "You need a break?"

"No. I need to get this out. Perhaps it can help with whatever is going on." She leaned against the dusty wall, rubbing her forearms. The room seemed to have dropped a few degrees, now that I thought about it. I gave a soft nod with a softer smile.

She continued, seeming to find comfort from the gesture. "There was a long, haunting silence, eventually broken by jumbled voices from every direction. Soon after, the hold melted away. My body didn't respond at first. A crumpled ball learning to breathe again. After a few hours, or even days... I don't know, it all blended together, I gradually regained the ability to move. First my head, then fingers, finally my limbs."

It sounded horrific. I tried to hide my expression, not to react as she relived the hell, living in a state of sleep paralysis lasting longer than humanly possible. I wanted to get moving, but found myself lost in her story, her fear. And maybe she was right, it might help—if she was telling the truth—the timing seemed too coincidental.

Her eyes narrowed, catching my agitation as thoughts vacillated between curiosity and the urge to find Quinton. "I'm holding us up. My backup auto should still be in the barn out back." And just like that, any vulnerability disappeared. She was done talking, whether it helpful or not.

I followed her outside, greeted by a fresh woodsy breeze. Pine trees surrounded the small cabin, the only exception: a clearing with a dirt road leading deeper into the greenery. The silence, broken only by the crunch of footsteps, was a welcome change from chaos and explosions. I inhaled deeply, the scent of pine strong in the earthy, humid air. The sky was beautiful—rain clouds almost giving way to clear blue with a hint of rainbow hiding between breaks of the treeline.

Lost in nature, a loud clunk pulled my attention back to Alycia throwing a heavy chain onto the dirt. "Some rush you're in. Help me out with the door."

From the outside, the shed had seen better days. Paint hung on for its dear life, chipping off the weather-worn lumber. The roof was in worse condition, several large holes in the shingles, many of which were scattered on the dirt perimeter. Alycia opened her hand, palm upwards, presenting the shiny, scuffed up barn door.

I dug away some rocks, hoping to clear a path before I wrapped my fingers around the door. A loud grunt escaped my throat as the steel sheet slid over and settled into a pile of small stones. Without hesitation, Alycia strolled in and flicked a light switch.

One fluorescent tube struggled—the only cooperating in the group of six—settling into a steady white glow, joining thin rays of sun pouring through holes above. Paper backing of insulation lined the barn, some areas appearing wet and moldy from months of unprotected rainfall. I dodged a puddle of water, almost tripping on the rocky ground.

"Ah, she's still here," Alycia said, beaming a soft smile while approaching the blue tarp wrapped over a set of wheels. "We're gonna need petrol. Grab a can from the cabinets while I check the engine."

Alycia tore off the tarp like a magician revealing a trick, accompanied by a "Ta-da", revealing a light yellow car. Memories from my car-loving celebrity self flooded through. It was a 73 Thunderbird with a 5.0 V8 engine. I didn't have to be a car enthusiast to know it was in rough shape. Scuffed, dinged, and with a large crack through the windshield, I debated ending the search for gas early.

Alycia circled the car, running her hand over the body while her smile grew larger. I hoped she knew what she was doing, the thing looked barely functional. I turned my attention to the cabinets, nestled dangerously close to a giant drum labeled "Flammable". I rifled through the usual assortment of tools, accessories, and papers, making a mess displacing everything in the overly dramatic search. After knocking over an empty kerosene lamp to the soundtrack of Alycia's snickering, I found a small canister collecting dust behind a jack. Before I grabbed the can, a folder caught my eye, papers spilling out of the green worn cover.

A faded black and white photo peaked from the top of the pile. Underneath, a yellow hued newspaper cutout took my attention. *Inspector John Hales Posthumously Commended.*

CHAPTER 20

A jarring clunk echoed from behind. "Lookin good!" Alycia said, her hands firmly on the rim of the car, leaning her head under the hood. She continued fiddling underneath, causing me to think twice about questioning the mechanic get-up earlier. Damn assumptions.

I turned back to the workbench, using the distraction to stuff the photos and clippings back into the folder. Luckily, the comically oversized pants I sloshed around in had another use. The giant pockets swallowed the folder comfortably and hid them from plain sight. What was she doing with these files? I needed to see the rest of the folder before making any more assumptions. From the preview, I knew I would need time alone to digest the contents.

"You okay over there?" she yelled, still hunched over, peeking out the hood. Damn, did she see me nab the folder?

"Oh, uh—" Thinking on my feet, I rolled up my sleeves, showing the mess of sticky tape and steel. "You got anything to break these cuffs?"

She did a double take and shook her head. "I'm not even going to ask, but I'll do you better." The topic change worked. If she saw the theft, she didn't acknowledge it, coming back from the other end of the barn dangling a small set of keys on her index finger. "This should do the trick."

"Kinky," I said, accepting the keys and beginning the painful process of tearing tape and arm hair off in quick pulls.

"Comes with the territory."

Deciding not to question the response, I focused on my burning forearms, rubbing them like it would take away the pain. To my surprise, the key worked, sending each cuff to the ground. I remember hearing cuff locks are universal, something that still sounded strange.

"Oil hasn't been changed in over a year since I was here, but it should still zoom," she shouted while slamming the hood shut. "Fuel is in the tanker next to you."

I filled the can, making several trips back and forth while learning this was her own personal hideaway. A backup of the Tempus safe house, something unknown to even them. I didn't press her paranoia, instead fighting my own mistrust creeping in. After the seventh trip, the tank was topped off. Unless the car had a leak, we could ride for hours.

She took the driver's seat, complete with crass remarks that I couldn't handle such a powerful engine. "So, where are we headed?" She adjusted the rearview mirror and settled into the seat, exhaling with relief.

"Unless you have a way to contact Quinton or Lotus, or even Vance..." I trailed off intentionally, adjusting the seat a moment to stall in hopes she had a response.

The silence was painful, lasting only a few seconds but feeling much longer. "Oh?" She started the car and clicked a button on the visor above. One of the walls lifted with the help of a noisy motor I hadn't spotted until now. "I didn't realize you were waiting for me. I told you earlier, the phone wouldn't do you any good." She pulled out of the barn and cruised down the dirt road, stopping before the clearing to turn and face me.

"I thought you were just being combative." I squirmed in the seat, finding it difficult to get comfortable.

"After I woke up, I called every number I remembered. Even the hotline. You remember that one, *don't you*?" A small smile punctuated her sentence. Most likely a nod to last year when I unknowingly called the Tempus answering service, in turn notifying every member to who and where I was.

I tried to play it cool, fighting the urge to defend myself. "Hey, if you call back a mystery dialer who keeps calling, and you get a prompt asking for a password, *and you* find this password in a barcode *on your body*... What was I supposed to do! It only made sense!"

"That's what happened, huh?" Sounds like someone wanted you to get caught then, I reckon."

She sounded genuinely clueless. And if she *was* telling the truth, that meant she was in the dark about the mysterious old Bank of England certificate that started the whole mess. I'd have to pick her brain on that later, now that she wasn't trying to kill me.

She swiped a strand of wig hair from her eye, fluttering lashes to blink back her vision. The world melted away, all color and sound draining except for what existed in the tiny cabin of the sports car. Time stood still —with my history, I questioned if it was literally or figuratively—until I realized I was lost in her eyes. My heart skipped a beat, the wave of electricity stopping only when it reached my fingers and toes. We unlocked our gaze, both pressing hard into our cushions as the world returned into focus.

I've been opposite the receiving end, watching others lost in these baby blues—an almost supernatural charm that helped get out of a few sticky situations—like maybe with the good doctor earlier. But I've never experienced it myself. It was exhilarating—life giving, a somewhat sexual ecstasy mixed with a loving embrace, yet no physical touch. Is this what the others felt? Wow. Some of the old vampire novels mentioned this sort of thing.

A hawk passed overhead, the shrill caw fading as it was obscured by the trees. I peaked at her from my periphery, catching her doing the same, much rosier than her usual complexion.

"So uh... The last time I saw Quinton and Melissa was at this gas station in the desert." My voice broke, nervously wavering. I pulled to loosen my collar, finding the sweater had plenty of room, nowhere near my neck. "It sank into the ground."

"Yeah," she whispered, nodding slowly, still locked on the dirt road ahead. "I know where that is. I can get us there in under an hour." She pursed her lips while easing off the brake, gently accelerating through the wooded corridor.

THE FREEWAY BECAME a two lane road. The scenery looked less industrialized and more rural with each passing mile. Or kilometer, as Alycia had announced minutes earlier, finally breaking over a half-hour long silence. I found myself bracing for the next *unlocking*, wondering when I'd be sent back to London to uncover more of my past. A past that felt more like a fantasy. A dream to escape from the stress of today. The familiar chill of spiraling into madness washed through my nerves, unable to take in the beauty and peace of the empty desert. I pressed my head against the cold glass, using the old engine's vibration to ground myself back to reality.

If I had learned anything from my decades on earth, especially with what I went through last year, the biggest lesson was to trust my gut. And to face my fears. And right now, I was afraid to be alone. Floating adrift again with no guidance, on the run, not sure who to trust. I leaned into the fears, propping my head away from the window to face her. Her calm, almost doll-like demeanor was a complete change of character from the Alycia haunting my nightmares. The terror from her and Lucian faded months after our run-in at the cemetery. They gave way to new fears: the silence that followed, not hearing from Quinton, or *anyone* for months. Tempus had dropped a bomb changing my world, only to ghost. And I was left finding my way trying to assimilate back into the world. Alone.

I watched her in stillness for moments before finding the softness in my voice. "Hey."

Her chin moved, just barely, eyes shifting in my direction. "Hey."

"Thanks for, uh, saving me earlier. Twice." I looked down, instinctively trying to maintain some bravado, or pride, despite the logical part of my brain finding it foolish.

Her jaw softened before releasing the tension through her shoulders. "I suppose I owed you." She turned again, slightly, our eyes almost meeting as we avoided full contact. "You're welcome."

We both shifted in our seats, finally finding some comfort to make room for the elephant between us the past sixty minutes. I decided to follow my gut further. "There's something I can't figure out. I keep running it through my mind and it doesn't make sense."

Her eyes narrowed. "Do tell."

CHAPTER 21

I recounted the meeting with Melissa and Quinton. The ride, crash, and abduction of Vance. Our mission to stop the day repeating and the mysterious woman in the middle of it all. How she knew me, thought I was in line with Lucian and wanted us both dead. She listened intently without interrupting. If not for driving, I bet she'd be scribbling down pages of notes. I told her everything, only leaving out my recent trips to London. After finding her folder filled with mysteries, I eagerly waited for a moment to study it alone.

Her face wrinkled, then an elbow propped on the driver's side ledge as fingers ran over a smooth chin. "They said you were the last resort? This has been happening over and over again?" She placed her hand back on the wheel. "We have to work backwards, then."

There it was again, *we*. It felt nice. It felt confusing. I thought back to Olivia—there was something so special about her. Something my soul needed and ached for ever since we met. And now there was *her*. Alycia made me feel a bit more complete. Minutes ago, sitting next to her in silence was enough to break from my usual descent into madness.

Thinking backwards... "Okay," I said. "The day was

already repeating without me in the picture. So if I'm not with Vance..."

"That agent," she said. "The woman, Mara. She was looking for Lucian, correct?" I nodded. "Vance has been one of Orchid's top trackers for years. She was clearly following him to get close to Lucian. Or was following Lucian himself until the accident."

"And now I'm the new variable. If I wasn't there..." I tapped my fingers together, clapping them lightly while the gears turned above. "If I'm not there, Vance is still captured. And Mara follows the trail instead of going after me?"

"Most likely. And we know the attacker wasn't after you, which creates even more questions. Anyhow, Mara would have followed Vance's captor—Lucian, we have to assume? As long as we can keep her away from Lucian, the timeline should be safe."

I hesitated, almost biting my tongue, but knew I needed the answer. "You... you know Lucian. Why would he want Vance?"

She turned fully, facing me for the first time since our moment outside the barn. The faintest touch of saline welled in her eyes. "I didn't think I had a choice, Jay. It was chaos. Pharaoh was more concerned with you joining Lotus. The others sat on their buttocks. Lucian came to me with a compelling argument and—" She paused, wiping away the speck of a tear. "I let my personal feelings get in the way. You took seven years from us."

"Unintentionally!" I chimed in even though it sounded like she had finished.

"I know that now." She pressed her palms hard into

the wheel, flexing and rolling her shoulders. "Lucian is power hungry. He wants Lotus done away with. Always has. Not sure how he came to be the leader of Orchid." She broke her gaze from the road, scanning the desolate landscape of sand and mountains. "Vance is the best tracker I've known..."

I swallowed hard, hoping I was wrong, not wanting to speak it into existence. "Lucian is going to destroy Lotus, isn't he?"

WE RETURNED to silence for the next five minutes. From a distance, the old gas station looked just how I'd left it almost twenty hours ago. I didn't need to be a crime scene expert to see a fresh set of tire tracks next to the barely visible markings Vance left behind. My eyes followed the tracks and stopped at a matte black SUV parked on the opposite side of the building.

Alycia cocked her head after noticing it too. With a slight cringe and narrowed eyes, she came to the same conclusion. "Quite busy for the middle of nowhere."

She parked a few feet away from the dusty old building. We checked the SUV first. Unlocked and empty.

Now with the help of the sunlight, I could see the convenience store was in worse shape than the darkness led me to believe. The bricks had scuff marks, some were missing, and the windows—were they broken before?

A gut punch of fear sucked the air out of my lungs. "Wait." The thud from the car door slamming shut muffled my words. Alycia was already walking up the entrance with a fearless saunter.

"Something's not right!" I stumbled to her side.

She pushed open the door and hesitated, looking around then propping up her chin, followed by two loud snorts of air. "You smell that?" She crouched to the ground and continued searching the floor, sifting through pieces of glass and items knocked from the shelves.

I watched over her shoulder—it looked like an earthquake hit the store. More snacks and knick-knacks scattered the broken, tiled floor than were on the shelves. Anything breakable was broken. Including the secret freezer entrance, the door wide open and fighting desperately to stay on its hinges. A step forward and a cool gust of air filled my nostrils carrying an aroma of... nothing. The opposite of an olfactory response. Senses told one story, but my brain was confused, conflicted, knowing *something* should be there.

I sniffed the air in every direction, searching to find something. "What is that?"

Alycia stood, spotting the open door in the corner and sighing. "This isn't good. I've only been this close to an epicenter once before."

My left ear went silent. Hearing faded in and out with the right. Vision flickered like a neon sign ready to die before returning. "Earthquake? Bomb?"

Alycia squinted, staring intensely at my lips. She pointed at her ear and shook her head. "*Wrong... time...ripping,*" she yelled, her broken voice muffled, like deep underwater.

She motioned to follow, passing the rows of empty shelves until we reached the now not-so-hidden freezer corridor. I fumbled around in the darkness, looking for a switch to give us some light. My fingertips were weightless, numb, only faintly feeling the jagged stone wall against my skin. I found and flicked at the switch—nothing. Left to continue with only the faint light from behind, darkness intensified with each step.

I followed close behind, nose struggling to work in bursts to get a whiff of her scent—a faded smokey rose mixed with motor oil—oddly intoxicating. She yelled something out before pausing but it was too late, I had walked into her. My chest bumped hard against her, almost knocking us both over. Luckily, she predicted my clumsiness and had been bracing for the impact. I peaked around her to see the faint reflection of light against the wall ahead of us—a dead end. Alycia stepped to the left and pointed to the floor. Only inches of ground lay between us and the vast black abyss. I sank to my knees and gazed into the rectangular hole in the floor, feeling a faint odorless breeze wash through my face before fading. I shivered imagining the fall, floating through the infinite darkness.

Lost in complete nothingness with limited hearing, palpitations were the only sensation in my body.

"Jump?" Alycia's words warbled in an auditory mess.

My mind rewound to earlier today, remembering Melissa's magic sinking building trick. I rose and yelled, hoping my voice would carry through whatever was blocking our senses. "Wait here!" I followed the light to backtrack to the store. Behind the now-shattered plexiglass barrier, I fought more blurred vision, seeing a row of five buttons, each labeled with unrelated characters. I pressed the button with a blue flower. To my surprise, the first time was a charm. The building rumbled and slowly descended into the ground. As the earth enveloped the storefront, the only source of light followed while the broken windows darkened. "Shit!"

I jumped over the glass-filled counter, slicing my palm in the process, then searched the floor for anything that could serve as a light source. Potato chips, Twinkies, condoms, nothing useful. I bent to my hands and knees and frantically sifted through the dusty shards of glass and debris, smearing blood on the tile while cutting my other palm. The building continued shaking, falling lower and lower, now with only a sliver of light from the top of the window shining through. Lighters! I tore open the package and pulled out a lighter and pocketed the rest. Again shrouded in complete darkness, the vibrations seemed even more unsettling, the pit of my stomach twisting, heart racing.

I palmed the lighter then paused—the loss of smell and hearing, hazy vision, the "epicenter" she mentioned. What if there was a chemical leak? Risk blowing myself up or stumble in pure darkness? I lifted the lighter, closing my eyes during the non-denominational prayer, then flicked it on.

CHAPTER 22

Aflame erupted from the gas lamp before settling into its familiar flicker. The lamplighter continued on, muttering something under his breath.

Tonight felt different. The distant chime of Big Ben, the same. The airy swirls of fog, the same. The faint smell of sulfur, manure, and oil—all the same. But the goosebumps on my forearms told another story.

Now an hour after midnight, the moon illuminated the bumpy street. The cramped, three story buildings lined both sides of the road, huddled together in a cold mass of brick and wood. Typically frequented by drifters, prostitutes, and drunkards this time of night, the alleys were eerily empty. Sofie's contact was right this time—no law or citizens to be found. Stillness lingered in the air, our footsteps amplified by the quiet.

Someone has been changing the patrols, Green confirmed at our last meeting. One of the few bits of information he provided. At least information relevant to our case. He seemed more concerned with his secret society and tales of time travel since his return. I still found it difficult to believe, despite the deep sense within. A moment of lucidity washed over once more—like my mind from 2008 screaming into a void hoping I'd hear. Convincing me this was real before thrust back to my thoughts, fully resuming the life as John Hales from London.

I stopped, turning to Sofie while pulling the long patchy overcoat tighter. I had paid a drifter handsomely, hoping to blend in better than with my usual prowling attire. "Ready?"

Her lashes fluttered, eyes mirroring back the excitement and reality of the upcoming night. "Ready." Her lips curled into a smile. She flattened out her dress, a dull red extending below her knees yet still bright enough to cut through the fog, if you were looking. We weren't going for subtleties tonight.

She continued without me, the sharp clack of each heeled leather boot echoing against the stone. We had decided she forgo comfort, her waist tightly cinched under a corset creating an unnatural hourglass shape. Her hair fought the breeze, trying to escape snug braids bound in a large red ribbon. Beautiful as ever. I saw fierce confidence in every motion, even as she pretended to be the naïve damsel in distress. I hung back in the shadows, back firmly pressed against the brick—wondering if The Butcher was waiting in some dark corner doing the same.

Don't get too close, she warned as we planned the outing. I was to stay back a minimum of one block, ideally two. I didn't like the idea of keeping her so far. The grisly murder scenes of mutilated women, parts scattered, blood spilled—I knew what he was capable of. And with the theory that he lured them away, I hated taking the chance he could end her at a moment's notice. But I knew what she was capable of, too. Her strength, both in mind and body, was more than any woman I'd seen in all of England. And she viewed me as backup, not part of her plan—something I failed to convince her of otherwise.

She turned down a corner, leaving me alone on the foggy cobblestone street. I added an urgency to my stride while maintaining the persona of a drifter, hoping to meld in the background in case he was watching. Tiny neck hairs stood on end just at the thought. The stalker stalking me, stalking her. I feigned a swig from the nearly empty bottle of gin, spitting the liquid back with one smooth motion while adding another stumble, rounding the corner.

I caught a flash of red through the smokey air, disappearing into an alley a block ahead. My heart sank again, something I hadn't grown accustomed to even though it must have been the twentieth time tonight. Deserted and even darker, the street was worse than previous nights. Several shops boarded, one showed signs of irreparable fire damage. Only two of the street lamps held a flame letting darkness and fog win a hopeless battle.

I scanned the streets, still empty. No signs of life, even in the darkened windows above the remaining buildings. The pit of my stomach rumbled. Anxiety and hunger joined forces to produce a shaky sensation, first my fingers, eventually creeping into my arms. I should have eaten. *But shoulds have no place in the House of Hales*, my mother would say.

Glass shattered in the distance. My eyes rounded into circles. Fingers trembling and weak, I lost hold of the gin. The bottle broke into shards, tiny pieces crunching under my boots. My pupils danced in the night, hoping to find the source.

"Ayeeee!" the hunched shadow bellowed, throwing his torn-gloved fist into the air in solidarity. Covered in dull rags, the vagabond belched loudly and resumed his lean against the boarded building. *Be alert John.* I needed a clear head. Anxiety was my friend right now—its cousin fear, my enemy.

I approached where I had seen Sofie last, or at least the red blur, which I prayed was her. Clouds drifted over the moon, sending beams of light briefly illuminating the dark corridor. The stench of rotten meat wafted in, causing me to recoil and wince. Footsteps echoed, the reverberation between buildings making it hard to decipher boots from heels. I dropped the cloak and raced toward the noise, reaching for my pistol while stomping with a steady cadence. The footsteps intensified and grew louder, the fire in my lungs singed from the icy air of every inhale.

Crack.

A sharp pang flared in my knee, throwing me off balance, propelled into a pile of old newspapers and garbage. I stumbled to my feet, ready to reignite the chase, until I saw it. A streak of crimson liquid reflected in the moonlight, the muted color of a bow crumpled like trash on the stone. My chest rose and fell with fury, eyes scanning every dark corner finding nothing.

A second crack of leather on bone exploded in my skull. And then darkness.

CHAPTER 23

I opened my eyes to the soft flicker. Not only was the air *not* flammable, but the lighter actually worked on the first try. I almost exclaimed something about it being my lucky day—before I stopped to relive it. A car crash, dodging bullets, falling off a cliff, being drugged, a helicopter chase, escaping an exploding mineshaft. Did I miss anything?

Jinxing myself, a gust of air extinguished the flame. Suddenly losing vision, *and apparently balance,* my left foot smashed into the right. While crashing down, the lighter shot forward like a bullet, softly clicking against something in the distance.

Well, at least my hearing seems to be back.

A soft crunch stirred before settling, leaving me alone in the darkness. Or so I hoped. Where was the driver of that SUV, anyway? We had searched the perimeter earlier. But without our hearing or smell, the strange, almost dissociative state made the search cursory at best.

An intense thud ahead had me moving to the freezers. Hopefully Alycia hadn't fallen into the hole with all the vibration—I wondered if she was spooked by the commotion until I stopped the thought. Why did she suggest *we jump*? I had described this place as a sinking gas station and she knew the directions without a map. Another point for mistrust—or paranoia. I pushed away the worry and flicked on another lighter, illuminating the corridor until I reached the end, Alycia nowhere to be found.

With a few steps further, I realized the hole was no more. So the sinking served a purpose other than the enigmatic—it lowered to connect the station to a staircase. The descent continued for minutes, seeming longer than the first visit. I finally reached the bottom, finding the familiar, long stretch. My flame faintly lit the hallway, helped by the yellow glow from the ceiling's emergency lighting. Unable to see more than a few feet ahead, it was still a welcome change from total darkness.

Past the bolted doors on each side, I crept closer to what I dubbed "the war room". The secret bunker-like setup seemed secure enough to withstand anything from above.

Pressing on—still no sign of her. Why didn't she wait? Both ears popped, the faint humming of machines and footsteps faded in. My sense of smell grew stronger, fully returning to savor the familiar earthy musk.

"Alycia?" I yelled at the emptiness, hoping her hearing was back too.

"Hurry up!" her voice trailed ahead.

The relief faded fast, giving way to the mistrust I had been battling after finding the envelope in her hideout. I hastened my pace, causing the flame to kiss the tip of my finger.

"Ow!" I dropped the lighter, waving my hand frantically.

After reassuring Alycia I was okay, I continued further

down the hall. Now closer, light poured out from the command center, or whatever you'd call the secret base. I raced to Alycia's side and joined her motionless stance in front of the giant monitors. After a deep inhale of air, I bent forward, propping hands on my knees. The sudden lack of energy was a shock, body still recovering from the damage earlier.

Taking a few more breaths, I stood tall. "What's going on..."

The monitors were shattered—a large body-sized crack in the middle—someone was thrown against it. The scenic window had been replaced by flickering static and a splash of blood, actively trickling into a pool underneath.

Alycia extended her hand, motioning to stay behind. "Be careful," she said, creeping around the desk to investigate.

I declined the order and took the other direction, following the trail of blood that began under the screen. The red droplets grew in size with each step, now large patches and smears leading to what would have been a dead end. Behind the person-sized hole in the drywall, I caught the gleam of a hidden, metallic door. Nearing closer, I carefully dodged broken chunks of the wall scattered about.

"Just like the other safe house..." I said the obvious aloud, examining the odd architecture of the false wall.

With another deep breath, I paused, hand on the doorknob. All my senses fully functional, now at a time I wished they weren't. "Something's behind here," I said, grimacing, not wanting to find out.

"This is... not good," Alycia said from my side, any hint of color drained from her face.

I turned the handle and slowly opened the door, bracing for what was behind while fighting the urge to close my eyes. Alycia shifted her footing, ready to pounce. The precautions weren't necessary. Inside the small room, Melissa's body sat slumped against a brick wall. Her chest and torso covered, still-wet blood oozing from the gash under her chin.

CHAPTER 24

A sticky film covered my hands. I felt around in the darkness, smearing the warm fluid across the bumpy cement ridges. I was on the ground. My vision faded in abruptly, heavy brown boots inches away from my face, upside down. The smell of death—blood and rot—thick in the air.

"A little underdressed for an *inspector*, wouldn't you say?" The deep voice rumbled from above. The badge made a soft clank, landing inches from my chin.

I craned my neck, unable to find the owner of the voice through the searing pain. My spine seized in position while fire seared through every nerve, eventually settling into a dull aching itch several layers beneath the skin. I opened my mouth, struggling to manage even wisps of air and faint coughs.

"Good, you can't scream." The boots drew further away, a jingle of metal clinked with each step. "Tsk. That means you can't call for the whore."

Was Sofie alive? The excitement quickly subsided, overshadowed by helplessness and fear. Sofie surviving was great news, but it meant nothing if he went after her next. The footsteps jangled closer, accompanied by heavy thuds as they splashed in the mix of rainwater and blood.

In one swift motion, fire ignited my scalp as clumps of hair held on for dear life, head pulled taut to face my attacker. An oily oval-shaped mug leered back, piercing dark green eyes studying carefully. He sneered, exposing brilliant white teeth, sharp points that seemed to glitter off the faint light. His clothing told a story of opulence and horror. The elegant black top hat hid most of his thinning brown hair. A midnight blue suit, tailored to accentuate a muscular build. Specks of pink coated an otherwise ivory button-up, more undoubtedly hidden by his suit coat. And that face... so familiar. I'd seen it somewhere, but the clothing was more formal for anyone I'd encountered in recent weeks.

The fingers relaxed, my head snapping hard to the ground in a warm pool. The sound of fingers rubbing together produced a rain of hair feathering down.

"Not supposed to be any bobbies out tonight." He stood, pacing back and forth again. "Nor bobbies dressed as beggars following whores."

A stupid smile crossed my face—a blend of chemicals sought to block the pain along with the realization—the detective work succeeded. A spot on profile of the killer. Rich, influential man in his early thirties. And still, the asshole was smart enough to catch me.

"Hmm, what's so humorous, *Hales*?" The boots splashed around some more. "I didn't pay good coin for this playground for you to come fuck it up."

Pain exploded in my abdomen causing me to roll to my back. The Butcher retracted his boot and paused, as if questioning whether to continue. Choppy exhales told me something was broken, maybe a rib or two. I was getting under his skin and I hadn't tried very hard.

Despite the pain, the new position jogged some power back to my extremities. Now able to wiggle my fingers and toes, I had a renewed sense of hope. Maybe I could get out of this somehow. Where was my gun? Quick glances caused an embarrassing realization—I hadn't even acknowledged the surroundings. A large, covered patio sprawled above blocking some of the moonlight. Familiar dark brick walls lined the adjacent alleyway. Good—we hadn't moved far. Unfortunately, that meant we were hidden, deep in the alleys off the main road. Not that it would have done much good. The streets were empty.

"What do I do with you, inspector?" The gaunt horror towered above, contorting his face while bobbing his head, likely imagining an assortment of grim scenarios. He wandered into the dense fog, quick movements becoming disorienting rather than just annoying. A loud crack of thunder bellowed in the distance, soon followed by the soft rapping of droplets on the patio roof.

I tested my core strength and pushed to sit up. Surprisingly, most of the pain had turned to numbness, although a strange leaking sensation bubbled inside my gut. Now sitting up, a harsh cough escaped, projecting bloody spittle in his direction. "How about you go fuck yourself, your highness?" It was a last resort, *but if I could get him irritated enough to slip up.*

The dark figure twirled from the fog, almost stumbling while leaning again to meet me. The long lanky fingers reached from the suit coat holding a painfully sharp, thin blade. "Not my type." He smiled, an eerie grin appearing to have more teeth than possible.

The blade playfully danced closer and swooped

below my chin. I sat motionless, which appeared to surprise him by the quiver of his lip and wincing eye. He stepped back and massaged his temple, embarrassed his show of power had failed.

"You think you're so smart? Dressed in rags while I sliced up that woman in there," he said, pointing to the splintering wood door further down the alley. A sinister smile extended toward his cheeks causing his eyes to bulge. My heart sank. "Yes, yes that's right." He flicked his wrist, drawing half circles in the air. "Side to side. She was alive when I left her, not that there was much for you to save."

I pushed away at the earth, arms too weak to rise more than a few inches before I plopped down, discouraged. Another roar of thunder, this time much closer, echoing throughout the alleyway.

"You're a sick man." I coughed, blood and spittle trickled down my jaw. "But you weren't that hard to find. God have mercy on whoever stops you. They'll be less kind than I." If I'm going out, I might as well give him something to fear, I figured.

The madman crossed his arms, almost nicking himself with the sharp blade before adjusting his stance. His head bobbed, eyes not breaking my gaze. He peered intently, lost in my pupils which I imagined looked as sharp as his own knife. A sudden, violent tremor led him to recoil. He stumbled back while forcing his vision to the ground. "Nice try warlock. Maybe I'll gut you and move yet again. This town's worn out it's welcome—"

The thunk of wood on bone bellowed from his skull.

He slumped to his knees. Eyes glazed over and still fixed on mine, I wondered if he actually saw anything at all. Another loud crack and the body crumpled to the ground. I shielded my face from the splash, the puddle of bloody rainwater and spit exploding with force.

Green stood tall, overcoat drenched from the torrent that poured above. He approached and extended a hand, soon realizing I needed his full support to rise. Wobbly, I made it to the wooden door and propped myself against it with both hands.

"We need to—" Heavy coughs followed by more shaky breaths interrupting my speech. "In here," I gasped, pointing before clutching my chest.

Green stepped over The Butcher's limp body, taking a moment to kick the blade far from reach. With his support, I shuffled to the side, my back pressed against the wall, mentally bracing for what would happen next.

His hand paused on the handle. The uncomfortable silence finally broke with an unsettling groan as the damp wood creaked open. Green stepped back while I hobbled beside, peaking over his shoulder to find moonlight illuminating a grisly scene.

CHAPTER 25

I dropped to my knees and cradled her head, brushing hair from her cheek. Once blonde strands appeared reddish, stuck to splotches of blood on her neck. I checked her wrist for a pulse—looking for any signs of life, not that I knew what I was doing. Still warm, barely. I carefully pried an eyelid open, the pupil showing no response, drifting toward the ground.

"Melissa! Melissa, come on!" I shook the limp body, casting red dots across the wall while thrashing her between my arms.

I turned to Alycia, who stood hovering behind my shoulder. "Help me! We need to do something!"

Her clenched jaw and squinted eyes remained unchanged as she shook her head slowly.

A rush of adrenaline and emotion took control. Disregarding Alycia's resistance, I pulled Melissa to the floor, hoping to perform CPR—anything to bring life into the fading heart. As I slid the body lower, I saw what the Brit was eying—the massive red pool, a loss too great for any human to withstand. I rose and stepped back, running blood soaked hands over my face and beard, the smell of iron now deeply embedded. The comically oversized pants stuck to my skin, covered as well—soaked in the blood of a woman who was alive and well just hours ago.

My voice trembled, barely audible in the small hidden room. "I was too late. We could have stopped this."

"You don't know—" A crash cut her off, thundering from the halls behind. "Damn it, they're still here!" Producing a gun I had been unaware of, Alycia turned and bolted down the hall with a speed I was all too familiar with. "C'mon, pity later!" she yelled from the corridor.

I pulled away from the bloody scene, slipping on the slick tile only to catch myself on a desk in the war room. A loud rumbling shook the earth, challenging my balance again, already fighting for stability in slippery shoes. I started the jog toward Alycia, now at the far end of the hallway climbing the stairs. Around me, doors rattled, the walls rumbling a symphony of steel. Motor oil wafted from the ceiling vents, fighting the coppery scent caked in my beard. I pressed on, sprinting until—a solid brick wall. A small red 'Caution' sign flush against it, warning of the crushing mechanical staircase that I watched rise out of view.

"Hey! You up there?" I screamed into the darkness overhead, hoping my voice could fight through the grinding cascade of metal.

"I'm going after the—" Her words faded, consumed by the echoes of the strange building's mechanics rumbling throughout.

I could only imagine how foolish it looked, staring up at the void, hoping to will the stairs down using my mind. Another rumble of thunder exploded and the noises abruptly stopped, forcing me back to a new reality. An aura of defeat washed over until I locked on to her message. *Pity later.*

After a deep sigh, I hummed a few bars of an oldie but a goodie, singing quietly to an audience of one. *"Alone again, naturally."*

The next hour was alluring to repress—although I wasn't interested in adding to the growing collection of memories locked away in my brain. After moving Melissa from the hidden room, I realized the safe house had the same setup as the last. The room, once her final resting place, contained a giant rusty iron ladder.

Sprawling upward, the first few rungs were slick with Melissa's blood, causing me to slip and smash my forehead on the way down. Warm droplets sprinkled below, joining the red pool left behind by the sweet southern girl. Luckily superficial, the trickle stopped after a few minutes of pressure.

Every movement was hampered by the giant oversized pants, making me wish I had kept the stinky hospital scrubs until spotting a duffle bag containing a change of clothes. Now dressed in a pair of regular sized, *albeit tight*, stonewash jeans and a button up flannel, the mission upward continued.

After climbing the rungs for what felt like a mile, I reached the top to a dead-end. The lever on the ceiling airlock clicked but didn't budge enough to open. The small keyhole was all that stood between me and freedom—and finding out what happened to Alycia and the horrors of the last hour.

With no imminent escape, the sense of urgency dissolved giving rise to excitement and adventure. I investigated each door in the hall, rifling through filing cabinets and lockers, searching for anything that could be useful or clues to what happened. Only three rooms were unlocked, the first two showing no signs of personalization. A bed, lamp, and desk, drawers filled with illegible papers. The third sterile dorm was a replica of the others, except for the coffee mug resting alone atop the sleek desk. The black ceramic cup shined in the low LED lighting, half full, or empty if I went off today's events. I grabbed the mug, instinctively studying it without a real purpose. A brown coaster initially stuck to the bottom, dropping to the desk showing a worn outline of Texas etched in the corkboard. Fighting the tightness in my chest, I pulled at the drawers. Locked.

I had one last place to check, filling me with sadness and dread.

I SWALLOWED hard and approached the body, resting peacefully under the computer desk of the war room where I moved her.

"I'm sorry," I choked out.

I extended my hands reaching forcefully, trying to create as much distance as possible from my torso. My head craned just enough to see. Slowly, I ran fingers through her clothes, her pockets, her sides. Dried patches of blood crunched as I twisted, trying not to touch her body during the search. I stopped, feeling something dense in a back pocket. My face contorted again, cringing even more while I dug into the wet clothing, retrieving a bloodied smartphone.

I shook the slick plastic, sending a small cluster of dark drops on the desk. Relief battled the sick feeling in my heart, making it difficult to rejoice that the search wasn't fruitless. I set the phone aside and continued the exam, gently tapping her body until finding a small leather necklace. I removed the band over her head, revealing a dangling lanyard, blood dripping from the plastic holder and the keycard it held.

I clasped her chilly hand, whispering a few words of thanks in Japanese that flowed out without thought as a tear trickled down my face. Despite only knowing her for less than a few days collectively, she had been an important part of my life—even if some of it had been a ruse. She would get a proper burial, or cremation, or something. I'd make sure of it.

After a sad attempt to clean the phone, I held my breath and clicked the power button. The screen came to life, asking for a pin code or face ID. Of course, Melissa's secret connections meant it was waterproof, or blood-proof, and had better tech than what 2008 offered. I shook my head then hovered the camera over her face. After a soft click, the screen illuminated to the home screen.

"Thanks again," I said out loud.

I scrolled through the apps. Pretty minimalist setup and 80% battery. The contacts were limited, but surprising. Alycia, Tempus, my bar. Then a series of letters and numbers reminiscent of the game Battleship: S44, L12, K1... The list continued. I searched until finally my lips curved into an apprehensive smile. Tapping the small green button next to "Q," I brought the phone to my ear, feeling the smooth surface on my cheek. Silence. I pulled the phone away to see *No Signal* before the display returned to the list of contacts. The smile faded. I sucked air through my teeth. How did she call anyone here?

The rest of the phone was fairly vanilla—no photos, no notes, only a Tetris clone and a music app. I looked through her collection: an assortment of ambient and hip-hop tracks. I turned up the volume on the OutKast double album, starting with *Prototype*. At least there were tunes. And I still had the keycard. *And the folder I stole from Alycia.*

The card ended up opening Melissa's room. Her actual room, despite my earlier assumption. While still a depressing, dark dorm, it was slightly bigger than the others and had a few trinkets, clothes, and a personal bathroom. On the large workdesk sat a computer, surrounded by several drawers I found were unlocked.

Fighting the initial, somewhat curiosity-induced urge, something inside said to respect her privacy. I vacillated between tearing through the drawers and the very real need to find a way out.

Temporarily avoiding a decision, I took a deeper dive into Alycia's files. Parts of the faded binder had soaked through with Melissa's blood, obscuring sections of the photos and newspaper clippings. I spread them across the desk and turned on a lamp, studying them intently.

Three faded photos. The first was of me. Well, Inspector Hales—about the same age as the recent memories. He, *I,* stood shoulder to shoulder with Green, both wearing cheap wool suits and slight smirks. My eyes widened, focusing behind them on the scaffolding wrapped around the newly constructed Statue of Liberty. The second photograph, even through the blood smears, distortion, and heavy brown beard, showed the sharp features of Hales. The crows feet and rough aged skin dated him a few more years than the last photo. On the back, beautiful penmanship drew several question marks to accompany the name Michael Green. The name sounded familiar, although generic. Crimson stained the third photograph. Underneath the smears, I made out the silhouette of a woman. In my eagerness, I scrubbed at it only to remove some of the ink and wear out the paper. I slammed a fist, rattling several more drawers open. Angry at myself. Angry at whoever killed Melissa.

After a few moments lost in still, eerie silence, the thunk of an air circulator kicked in. I continued, finding two newspaper clippings under the photographs. Both appeared to be printed from a local library's microfiche, copies of a copy.

The first header: *John Hales Spearheads Taskforce.* The short blurb featured a picture of Hales, Green, and two other local lawmen gathered in a town hall setting. It introduced Hales as a newly promoted investigator sent from the big city to track a serial murderer. It tracked with the memories, but didn't provide any new information. I brushed aside the article and picked up the other clipping—which I was both awaiting and avoiding.

Written a month after the first, the article started: *Visiting London Inspector John Hales was commended posthumously for his bravery, found drowned earlier this week.*

CHAPTER 26 

"Dear Lord, the monster..." Green shook his head and knelt in front of the body.

I followed the pool of blood to the woman slouched against the wall in the tiny vestibule. The once-ivory evening gown was now soaked and had turned scarlet. Blood cascaded from the deep smile carved in her throat. Lashes twitched, open eyelids revealing pupils rolled back into her skull. The shock faded for a moment with the realization—*It wasn't Sofie.* Relief, then guilt for having relief coursed through my nerves.

Green put a hand near her mouth, feeling for any signs of life. With his other hand, he nestled her head and whispered. "You're safe now. He can't hurt you or anyone ever again."

The corner of the young raven-haired woman's mouth twitched upward. Maybe the softest death throes, or what we wanted to believe instead—she understood. All movement stopped. The lifeless woman sank delicately to the side.

Green released his hold and stood, looking at his blood-soaked hands then back to the horror. "Even after seeing so many bodies, I'll never get used to this." He turned and looked over his shoulder out the door. "Good thing I won't have to."

The Butcher's body remained motionless next to the baton used to club his brain. Through the dim rainy moonlight, I caught the faintest movement in his chest, rising and falling. "He's still alive."

Green surveyed the dark alleyway, sniffling in the chilly air. "Not for long."

Forego a trial? Despite my anger, fear, and remorse, I hesitated. I wanted to murder this killer myself—the man who had no scruples doing the same. But what would that make me? I wondered if my thoughts would change had Sophia's body lay in front of us.

The tall man scratched his bushy beard, watching the moral dilemma, then placed a calming hand gently on my shoulder. "We have another problem, John." He walked around the grimy backstreet, picked up the blade, then searched the killer's clothing. "The man I told you of..."

And just like that, the lawman switched gears, tearing me away from the sick reality we had just experienced. The culmination after weeks of police work, the most gruesome murders in London, the highlight of my career. And there he was, searching the murderer while explaining that the mystery man he warned of had caught wind of my existence.

"I don't know how he knew it was you. He saw the article of your promotion, your arrival a few weeks ago." Green rose, clutching a second, smaller knife and a thick pack of bills secured by a silver money clip. "Rich bloke, wasn't he?"

I leaned on the wall, wishing for a tobacco pipe to

distract from the confusion. "He said something about paying for all of this." I massaged a knuckle through my scalp, surveying the damage to my head. "He was paying someone off to change the shifts."

"Williams, no doubt." He thumbed through the money, frowning. "I discovered he was the final say in the patrols. For a man that's been hands off, it's quite suspect. And after he suddenly pulled coverage from this area at the last minute, well, I suppose great minds think alike, Hales."

The back of my head throbbed. A wave of nausea swept through causing a lightheaded sensation. I doubled over and heaved several times. A small trickle of bile escaped onto the cement. "This mind isn't doing so hot right now." I wiped spit away and leaned back against the wall. I wanted to lie down and sleep for days, but the twitching body and Green's cryptic message warned there was no time for rest.

"What now?" I pointed my chin at The Butcher, his arms beginning to stir.

Green noticed the movement and landed a swift kick in the killer's skull. The stirring stopped as he settled back into the faintest signs of life. "I'll take care of Williams. Give me your badge."

THE PLAN WAS OUTLANDISH, but it seemed the safest option given the danger Green outlined. After dressing The Butcher in my clothes, gun, and badge, we heaved him into the River Thames. The cover of night and knowledge of police patrols helped us dodge any unwanted attention. Just two men out for a stroll with their drunkard friend.

Despite my earlier guilt, returning visions of each bloody scene haunted every step with the madman perched on my shoulder. Each life he stole. Every husband, father, mother affected—the families he tore apart. The cloud of fear covering the city for months. Watching his still-breathing body wrapped in the cold, dark water—I no longer felt guilt. I felt vindication.

The unconscious body slowly disappeared as the watery grave welcomed its guest. His face battered beyond recognition and hair torn to shreds, Inspector John Hales ended his life in pursuit of a robber, Green would later announce after the corpse rose to the surface.

"I have a friend at the paper." His eyes followed the cool waters while they settled into their usual ripple. "I'll make sure the news gets out about your death. And heroism."

"Are you sure that will be enough for him? Won't he come looking?"

We began our walk toward the city with Green leading the way. "Sure? No, I can't be sure of anything. But when he questioned, I played dumb. I told him I believed my connection to you was a dream. That gave me another chance. He said he would come here to take care of you." He paused, glancing at the water behind, now a block away. "That solves that."

"Aren't you forgetting something? I can't just pretend to be someone else!"

"Not here you can't." Green smiled, pulling out a small envelope. "Here you go, Michael."

I stopped to tear it open. Money and a birth certificate reading *Michael Green.*

"You'll need it for the boat, brother," Green said.

Through the haze of sickness and terror, I hadn't even questioned the endgame of his plan until this moment. "You mean..."

My new brother filled the pause. "I've booked us a trip to America. New York City, to be exact. Discreetly. *On the record,* we are headed to the Orient. To throw anyone off in case they are watching."

I held the birth certificate, staring at a tear in the paper. "America?" I broke from the daze and looked over at Green. "What about Sofie!" I trembled, tears welling in my eyes. The words spilled out. "She's out there somewhere! I found her bow, he said he—"

Green grabbed my head forcefully, clenching with his palms. "Listen to me. Your new life starts now. John Hales is dead. Whatever you had with her is over. If she knows anything, you both are dead." He let go and pulled closer for a hug. "I'm sorry it has to be this way. I'll make sure she's okay."

I cried in his arms as he ran a finger through my hair, letting the tears soak his shoulder. While *legally* his brother, I felt him more of a father in this moment. I pulled away and wiped the saline. "Thank you. For everything."

A gentle smile curled in the corner of his mouth. "Time to see the land of opportunity. That's what the Yanks still call it, don't they?"

CHAPTER 27

A loud thunk caused me to jump and smash my knee into the desk. I leaned down to massage it, something shimmering catching my eye. Deep in the back of Melissa's desk drawer was the key to my escape. The soon-to-be bruise would be worth it, after all.

The heavy steel airlock slammed shut after I said my goodbyes to the bunker below. From the outside, the unassuming tan colored panel marked "Utility" gave no indication of the secrets it held underneath. No coincidence, it easily blended with the sandy desert ground.

I rolled my shoulders then stretched in the blazing sun, hoping to ease my muscles from the long climb. After a short time, my vision adjusted to the bright desert expanse, mountains far in the distance with nothing in their path. A kilometer behind stood the gas station. I began the uneventful walk when my pocket vibrated.

The cellphone! Luckily I had thought ahead and reprogrammed the PIN before leaving. A missed call from "Q". The voicemail showed it was about four hours old. Finally, *something*. I hoped for good news, but any information was good news at this point.

Quinton's voice was hushed but clear. "Hey Mel. You

were right about the Vegas safe house, it's torched. Certainly reads like the self-detonation protocol was used. Police here are saying a John and Jane Doe entered right before it exploded. I'm going to check out the exit and follow up. Be careful and call me as soon as you can. I have a bad feeling."

So Quinton was hot on my trail, just a few hours behind according to the timestamp. I called back, only getting a generic voicemail prompt. "Hey, call me back if you get this."

Hopefully he was still alive. I repeated the same process with Alycia and even tried a few of the random numbers, opting only to leave a message for her. The Tempus hotline and Cartoon Graveyard were both disconnected. Things seemed headed from bad to worse. I scrolled through the call history. Melissa received a call from Q a little after nine. She then made two calls to him about an hour after. The calls averaged around two minutes each. A bad feeling indeed.

I burst into a jog, closing in on the gas station. No sign of Alycia's car or the SUV. A new set of tire tracks led away, joining the bumpy two lane road in the distance. From the curve, they headed east—thus beginning the long trek. I trudged for over thirty minutes in solitude until spotting the first car. With thumb raised to the sky, I chuckled to myself while the small blue Ford Focus slowed and pulled onto the shoulder. The window rolled down to a medium build white man with shaggy brown hair and a neat goatee. Catching my reflection in his dark, orange-brimmed eighties-style sunglasses, I looked like shit. But at least I wasn't covered in blood.

The man adjusted his rearview mirror before speaking. "Didn't think I'd see anyone out here. Where ya headed?"

He didn't sound like a serial killer, but his style was definitely eccentric. Teal and purple zig-zags like the ones found on old paper cups adorned his t-shirt, above it a green and white beaded choker wrapped around his neck.

"You okay?" he asked with a hint of suspicion cutting through the silence.

I coughed and attempted a warm smile. "Yeah, sorry. Been out here a while. Car broke down a few miles back."

He squinted faintly enough to see behind the grey lenses, then scrunched his face like the sun still bothered him. "Hop in," he said with less enthusiasm. "Vegas is just ahead."

THE SHORT RIDE WAS MEMORABLE, for me, more so than him.

"What's your name, buddy?" he asked, turning the air conditioner to a higher setting even though it was already quite comfortable.

I paused for only a moment, but he seemed to note. "My name's Clay. Bill Clay."

He nodded and tried to hold back a smile, looking away to his mirrors as a distraction. "Okay. I'm picking up what you're putting down, Johnny Boy." He chuckled, then coughed to cover it up. Clearly he saw through the action movie pseudonym. "The name's Paul. Paul Washington," he said, pausing before continuing with a different expression. "Hey, have we met before?"

Then it hit me. The retro getup and cartoon cat doll suctioned to the window, among other toys and fake Flux Capacitor, had all been a hell of a distraction. I was sitting next to Paul Jackson—the name I once knew him by. In a distant, now alternate-future, he was the co-star in my celebrity biopic. He looked much healthier than I remembered, not only six years younger—he had a glow about him. A zest for life I never saw on set. He had struggled with addiction and depression in secret, made worse from stressors of the business.

The glimmer of happiness created an overly exaggerated smile. It was the first time I felt l could make something better after setting the world back seven years and running through the motions. I was told not to mess with destiny, but maybe, just maybe, this interaction could have a positive effect.

Getting to know Paul in his early years was a nice chance of pace from the constant running of the past day. I'd learned he was a wanna-be private investigator from Detroit on a wild hunch that brought him to the deserts of Nevada. My initial fears of his profession subsided after I let him talk, partially tuning him out as he rambled about his case while going on tangents full of eighties and nineties pop-culture references. Either he was too wrapped up in his own mysteries, or my face wasn't plastered all over the news from the explosion and crash. From his excitement, I imagined it was a combination of both.

As we neared a small dusty motel, the Vegas skyline hovered into view. My skin tickled in the way I had heard people describe an allergic reaction. The undeniable pull

I'd experienced several times earlier—I needed to get out.

"This is my stop!" I called out.

Paul cut the wheel and skidded into the sandy parking lot without breaking a sweat. I got the impression he loved living out the excitement of the unknown. Or recreating eighties action flicks. Before I escaped his moving toy store, he gave me a business card emblazoned with the bright, colorful squiggles and shapes of a Memphis pattern, his name underneath.

I tucked it in a pocket, hoping I'd never have a use for it ever again. "Good luck on your case, bud. I can tell you're a great detective."

"Hey man, thanks. It was nice meeting you," he said from the open window. "Your friend, in time." He smiled and shot me a finger gun before flicking down his sunglasses and driving onward, almost losing traction on the rocky, unpaved ground.

I shook my head and grinned, watching his Focus putter away past the lot and—Alycia's car. Relief spilled over me enough to raise my fists to revel in the small victory. The joy was short-lived. Parked two spaces over was the matte black SUV.

CHAPTER 28

I attempted a slow, unassuming stroll past the motel rooms, briefly pausing to leer through each window. If anyone was watching from the outside, they would have seen the most suspicious peeping tom, not a formerly renowned London investigator. Luckily, this desert stretch to Vegas was the road less traveled.

A gust of wind threw sand into the air, causing a battle between man and nature. After wincing past a few more empty rooms, I froze—through the partly closed horizontal blinds I caught the blur of gold hair. I took a step back and leaned against the door, adjusting to get a better view.

Obscured by not only blinds, through the smudged, grimy window, Alycia leaned against a desk in the far corner. Her butt acted as a cushion, bracing her body while her hand rested beneath her other elbow, arm extended and aiming a pistol across the room. She wore a look of deep thought, an eyebrow raised briefly before gently nodding her head. The gun rose, ultimately used to brush away loose strands of hair. Her casual body language seemed to imply this was business as usual.

I crept closer, careful not to make any sudden movements. Alycia's fixed gaze allowed easy passage past the window, gaining a new vantage point. Opposite her sat Mara, arms stretched behind and wrapped unnaturally around a wooden chair. Alycia sauntered forward and leaned close, muttering something in the captive's face. After stepping back, the pistol hovered carelessly near Mara's torso. Although the one sided conversation was muffled, I didn't have to be a detective to recognize this was an interrogation. Through Mara's watery, darting eyes and rapid breathing, it seemed clear—the normally fearless agent had no answers. The newly duct tape-free mouth appeared to say, "I don't know." Or "Nintendo", the latter from Paul's influence still lingering. And I doubt that warranted the vicious pistol whip she received next.

Mara's head slumped for several seconds. She regained consciousness, her neck visibly straining as she fought to regain control. Sporting a new forehead gash, she winced while a small stream of red trickled down her cheek onto her black polo. Alycia paced in and out of view, gun tapping against her thigh. I pulled away, taking cover from the window.

Did Mara kill Melissa? She seemed consumed with ending me, and her partner came dangerously close to doing the same. I felt queasy. Call me a fool, but I didn't think the agent was to blame. Slit throats didn't seem like her style—if there was such a thing for murder. Reading Alycia's body, it appeared she didn't share my doubts. I couldn't watch Mara die or stand by idly knowing it happened.

I swallowed hard, hoping to push down whatever was rising in my throat. *I can't let this happen.* My mission was to *find* Mara—if Lotus wanted her dead, wouldn't they just tell me? It was obvious—Alycia wasn't following orders. This was personal.

I propped myself from the brick wall and shook my hands, getting some juice flowing to prepare for the unknown. About to rush in and—my pocket vibrated. The surprise caused a sharp exhale from my nostrils as a soft, generic jingle gradually rose in volume. Shit. I sank back against the wall and slithered in the other direction. Hopefully I hadn't blown my cover—although a distraction might buy Mara some time. A glance at the phone showed an incoming call: one of the strange combinations of letters and numbers. Curiosity won. What's the worst that could happen? I accepted the call and pressed the phone to my ear. "Hello?" I whispered, now loitering in front of the next room.

"Jay? Is that you?" Quinton's rapid voice turned the question into more of a statement. A frustrating, drawn out sigh lingered before he continued, "They got to her, didn't they?"

"Yeah. It's bad." I swallowed again, sending thick saliva away.

"Pharaoh too. Where are you?" His voice was devoid of emotion, almost callous.

"I'm—" I cut myself off, watching Alycia pace around the room. A wave of uncertainty washed over. For the first time in months, doubt slithered back into my mind. I felt an unbreakable bond with Quinton, only stronger by fresh memories of Whitechapel. But here I stood, saved by the enemy. And she appeared to be preparing to avenge Melissa's death. What if I had it all wrong?

"Are you still there?" Quinton said. A car door

slammed in the background causing a wince. I was on edge.

"Yeah. What the fuck is going on, *Quinton*?" I punctuated his name with an explicit sharpness.

"Jay, I'm flying blind right now. Did you find the woman? And how did you know about the Vegas safe house?" He sounded sincere, but the creeping doubt and confusion was difficult to shake.

"I'm looking at her right now."

"Good, we need to keep her safe," Quinton said as I watched the gun waved near her forehead.

My tone was harsh and direct. "Why?" It was becoming clear he was holding back information.

"If she dies, it's possible we'll go through this all over again. Maybe we've even had this exact conversation before, but I'm willing to try. You need to break the cycle."

A new thought burrowed its way through the shock and trauma of the day, obvious in hindsight. I slinked away from the window as the volume of my voice increased. "Don't you want a chance to save Melissa? Pharaoh?" I didn't want Mara to die. Hell, I was ready to jump in and save her before the call. But another crack at the day was alluring. "If the day resets, can't we save everyone? Why wouldn't we want that?"

Another exasperated sigh from the phone. "We're in uncharted territory, Jay. Tempus... murder isn't common among us. We are hard to kill, but we are not immortal. I'll explain later." A long pause floated by like the empty potato chip bag rustling in the breeze. "Hagaki, are you listening?"

The words registered, but I was frozen, speechess.

Alycia twisted the silencer and aimed, ready to fire at her hostage.

CHAPTER 29

Alycia wouldn't shoot me, right? At least she couldn't kill me, but it sure would hurt.

I mumbled something to Quinton before pocketing the phone and knocking on the window, waving and wearing a shit-eating grin. She approached and paused. And then the blinds closed. Damnit. Maybe not the best approach, but I banked on the last few hours we had together. And working some of that awkward former celebrity charm.

Faint rustling bled through the door before it swung open. Alycia stood wearing a scowl, eyes narrowed. "I found her. You don't have to see this."

I peaked over her shoulder, locking eyes with Mara, now gagged and still bound to the chair, silently pleading for help.

"Let me in."

Alycia squinted, reading the seriousness on my face, then stood aside. "Come, quickly now."

Three quick steps and the door slammed shut—Alycia pressed against it, gun pointed outward. I was close to the hostage, partially blocking the shot. *Unless she was aiming at me, too.*

"Move out of the way. She knows too much."

"You can't kill her," I stated matter-of-factly while hoping to hide the fear. Her bullets might not be fatal, but that didn't quell the panicked thoughts racing within.

"She knows too much," Alycia repeated. "And she was there when Melissa..." Was that a flicker of sadness? She brushed it off and continued. "Get out of the way and let me take care of this."

I didn't budge. "Remember our conversation? You said it yourself. We have to keep her away from Lucian to protect the timeline—"

She interrupted, the sharpness of her British accent cutting through. "We *are* keeping her away from Lucian if I kill her. And this is protecting all of Tempus. Move aside."

"You don't *really* think she killed Melissa, do you?" I pointed back at Mara. "She was just following your old buddy!" The captive's head nodded in agreement.

"Why are you protecting the woman who tried to kill you? And what would you propose? We just let her free to carry on about her life—"

"Like Olivia?" It was my turn to interrupt. "She was an outsider thrown into this. She's out there somewhere, probably confused and scared."

Frustration evident, Alycia shook her head, eyes rolled in annoyance. "You're a fool if you believe that. Now step aside. This is your final warning. In case you forgot, the bullets *will* hurt. And she'll still die."

A fool? What did she know about Olivia? Alycia wasn't in the information giving mood and was primed to follow through on her promise. And here I thought we were starting to hit it off.

Time for the last resort—I put my last card on the table. "What about John Hales?"

The harsh expression softened. With a slight tilt of her chin and narrowed eyes, the pistol drifted a few inches toward the shaggy carpet floor.

I saw the opening and cautiously approached. "Why are you looking for him?" The gun was almost within an arm's reach.

Anger blazed in her irises. "What do *you* know?" The weapon rose again as she adjusted her posture, shifting into a shooting stance.

Well shit, that didn't work. Let's try something new. "I know he faked his death. Ran away to America to avoid getting caught."

Her eyes widened, arms fully relaxed as the gun pointed back to the ground. Bingo.

"How do you know this?" Her stare intensified, focused on my face, my eyes. And not on my hand, grabbing her gun and training it back on her in one smooth motion.

"Sorry," I said, exhaling after smacking her in the temple. She fell harder than I expected, smashing her forehead on a sofa chair before the ground. A narrow trickle of blood dripped from the newly formed cut. From behind, muffled noises escaped through the gag.

Watching Alycia's body curled on the floor, I couldn't help but shake my head in sympathy. I felt sick, even though she would fully heal in minutes. Minutes I needed.

"We don't have much time. Let's get these off you." I looked around, hoping to find something to cut the captive's restraints. No luck. Instead, my hands danced like they knew what to do, unknotting the rope with ease. "I'm not going to hurt you. We need to get out of here, fast. Before she wakes up."

Alycia groaned from below, thankfully still unconscious.

"I'm going to take this out now," I tried to say calmly. "Don't scream. Please trust me." With the gag off, Mara inhaled deeply, chest heaving and body trembling. Her eyes darted up to mine, briefly lost in the sea of blue—comes in handy sometimes.

I GRABBED both sets of car keys from the dresser and decided on the Thunderbird. It was more my style and I didn't want to chance Alycia having a spare key. Mara complied with my sharp commands, trusting her newfound savior for the time being. She looked groggy, likely adding to her compliance.

The car roared to life before it skidded on the dirt path. Now stabilized on an actual road, we raced toward the skyline of Vegas hotels. Despite landing a knockout blow and taking her keys, I continually scanned the mirrors, relief each time they were empty.

The interrogation left its mark. Mara's head sported a gash, dried blood under her hairline. I wondered how long they were in that room before I arrived.

After a few minutes of listening to the wind, she finally spoke. "What the hell just happened back there?"

I let out a faint chuckle and racked my brain for a response. "Where do I even start?" I stole a quick look at her and set my eyes back on the road. "Let's clear something up—I'm not a terrorist. Lucian isn't either." I stopped to laugh again. "Well, maybe he is. I honestly don't know, but we are *not* on good terms. He almost killed me last year."

I heard a *hmph* from the passenger seat with the crunch of leather as she adjusted to face me for a clearer view. "Yeah? Well, he *killed* my friend. My mentor." From the sound of her voice, I could tell she was looking away. "Lori was on to something. She linked the fucker to a dozen terrorist cells around the world. And then, poof, she disappears. But so does he. And every lead becomes a dead end. So I drop everything to find the asshole. Nothing. Radio silence for months and then yesterday, he pops up."

I caught a glance of her waiting, an unsaid implication: my time to talk. The conversation was jarring—sharing information when hours earlier she was hurling bullets. But there she sat, cool as a cucumber like I was her long-lost friend. Through the chaos of our escape, I failed to recognize the strange pull I had to her earlier, which I fully realized now. Did she feel it too?

I wasn't ready to give just yet. "Okay," I said. "Why did you try to kill me? Twice, if my hazy, waterlogged memory is right. Three times if I count your partner."

"He didn't!" She exclaimed, a bit too cheerful for my liking. "After all that lecturing about my use of force. I can't wait—"

I cleared my throat loudly, interrupting her tangent.

"Sorry," she said. "I get it, I owe you. You saved me back there. But you're leaving something out. I told you earlier, sounds like your memory *is* fried. During my search for Lucian, guess whose name comes up? Rich uncle Quinton and Jay fuckin' Bialy. Or Hagaki, whatever." She took a pause to suck air through her teeth. "Nice bar, by the way."

Then it hit me. My brain drifted to the summer. A group of sorority girls coming in for an end of semester celebration. Karaoke night. Her hair was longer, twisted in two big braids past her shoulders. She sang a song or two. Even though they were top 40 hits, I still had an ear for talent from a life in the music biz. She was good. Like, *really good*. More memories flooded back. When she stepped on that tiny makeshift stage, the voice I heard was so different from the one chatting up pledge sisters earlier. Raw, the kind of voice that could move emotions. Hints of a young Erykah Badu and she was giving a free concert.

Her talent was lost on that crowd. Like her boisterous friend who hogged the mic most of the night. She took much of my focus, obsessively going on about my buddy's latest CD. Well, a buddy from an alternate future, that is.

The group eventually had too much so I cut them off. Called a cab and they headed back to the dorms. Or so I thought. Now thinking back, she was overly curious about my family. Few pry deeply into my history while tending bar, but I wrote her off as being tipsy, or even flirting.

I looked over to see a devilish smirk.

"Damn. You're good," I said, bobbing my head while reliving the music from that night.

The smile reached further to the corners of her cheeks. "It's part of the job."

"No. Your voice. It's—"

"Enough!" A glow of rosiness developed on her dark

complexion. She sounded nervous initially, soon regaining her composure and rushing to fill the silence, leaving me off the hook to talk. "We'd been tailing Lucian and lost him. Hour later, miles away, we get a report of a hit and run. *And a kidnapping.* Matched his ride. And when we get there…" She shook her head. "Some coincidence finding you. When I realized it was you, and fleeing the scene…" Her voice trailed off, decreasing in volume, until continuing. "Well, I assumed it was either infighting, or you'd had a falling out with the prick. He takes your hostage and leaves you for dead or prison."

"Wow!" I blurted out. I couldn't help holding it in. "I guess I can see your perspective, but holy shit. What a story. And it's *completely* wrong."

We passed a sign announcing Las Vegas was 5 miles away. Through the aura I felt around Mara, there was something else. Something that became stronger with each mile toward the hovering towers of the city. From her expression of awe—she must have sensed it too.

We drove in silence for the next few minutes. My mind wandered, trying to piece together the day, revisiting the theory from earlier. If it wasn't for the crash, Mara would have kept following Lucian. Without me involved, would he still capture Vance? The tracker must have been the key, leading him to the gas station.

I cut through the stillness lingering in the air. "Hey, this might sound kinda funny. Have you been having any weird dreams lately?"

My eyes shifted to see her grimacing, nervously nodding her head.

CHAPTER 30

The horn caused us both to jump. The light was green, closely matching the nail polish on the middle finger belonging to the driver racing by. After breaking free from the shock of the horn, *and Mara confirming the strange dreams*, I pulled into an empty parking lot. The barren construction site was a ways off the strip, but had signs announcing the future home of the Starlight casino and resort.

Several beads of sweat rolled down Mara's forehead. They combined with blood to cause a glistening red droplet dancing on her cheek. She wiped it away and cleared her throat.

"So," she started, followed by fake laughter and an overcompensating low-pitched voice. "How'd ya know!" Clearly using humor to avoid the discomfort. I understood—it wasn't my first rodeo having the weird-dream conversation.

"Tell me." Now parked, I had turned to face her with my full attention.

She traded her grin for a raised eyebrow after seeing my stone face of seriousness. "Wow, okayyy. Last night..." She swallowed hard and turned to look out the windshield. "I had this dream that I was tailing Lucian. I followed him for a while, through the desert. At some point, it was pretty obvious. He had to know. We were the only cars on the road but we kept going."

I waited for more, but she sat forward, lost in thought. "That it?"

Her head bobbed, squinting and blinking her eyes, likely trying to bat away visions. "Ugh. Well, I just remembered. It doesn't really make sense. Dreams, ya know?" Another nervous chuckle from the agent. And yeah, *I knew.* "I feel like I kept waking up and falling back asleep. But every time, I kept reliving that dream. A little different each time." She shifted to face me. "Shitty night of sleep." Her shoulders raised into a playful shrug. "Work has been on my mind a lot lately. What can I say?"

I couldn't help but narrow my eyes, reading the too jovial expression that was beaming from the passenger seat. "You're not leaving something out, *are you?*" I also couldn't help adding some punch to the question.

She jerked away and ran a hand through her hair, lightly pulling and twisting at the short orange spikes. "That weird gas station you were at, with that woman..."

"You were hiding somewhere in there, weren't you?"

"In the stockroom. I knocked over a bunch of shit trying to hide, but it didn't make a peep. You were both so disoriented when you walked in. Odd now that I think about it, I started feeling sick when you pulled up."

"It was in your dream, wasn't it?" We were finally getting somewhere. Where, I still didn't know.

"The last thing I remember before waking up... I pulled a gun on Lucian outside a place like that. I think he returned fire." She winced, fighting the brief, full-bodied tremor. "Yeah. Something like that."

She died in her dream. *Dreams*. Over and over, if what Quinton and Melissa had been going on about was true.

It was real. The loop the world had been stuck in. I sighed and tapped my fingers on the cracked leather steering wheel in thought. The strange sensations we experienced at the station. Alycia mentioned an *epicenter*, offering no explanation. I shuddered, imagining the fabric of time was tearing. Wearing away with each hard reset, occurring at the same time, the same place. How long could this keep happening? Keeping Mara alive suddenly became even more important.

I recalled my own experiences, back to Green's story in the pub. Death, or at least near-death, was the catalyst. The carriage fall in London. His own brush with the day repeating. Later my dreams from 2014—the last memory, that shady record producer Terrance pulling the trigger and—bam, back on the bus to Cali before I was famous. And each time after, weird things happened, strange characters emerged.

So Mara was like me—or on her way to it, but blocked? Why did the day loop when she died instead of sending the clock back? I wished I ignored Quinton's phone call. Living the same day over in ignorance sounded really appealing right now.

A hand waved into view. "Hey, you alive in there?" I turned to respond with a quick nod. "You kinda zonked out there for a minute. What's going on?"

"I was really hoping that talking to you was going to help me figure that out."

"Not so much I take it?"

"No. But I need to get you somewhere safe for now. I've got to call a friend. Stay in the car."

She complied, despite the confused look on her face. I didn't want to take the chance that *something* strange would happen—like with her partner earlier. I took a few steps from the Thunderbird and redialed Quinton's number.

"I was getting ready to call you," he answered. "I owe you an apology."

"Later," I interrupted. "I'm with the woman of the hour right now. She's safe." A truck whizzed by uncomfortably close, throwing me off balance momentarily. I walked to the other side of the car onto the shoulder, taking note of the beautiful sun beginning to set on the horizon.

"Before you hung up earlier, I could have sworn hearing something about Alycia?"

I filled him in on my rescue from the hospital, the explosion, and the return to find Melissa. He listened in silence, finally responding after I explained the interrogation.

Quinton's voice was more gravely than before. "I never understood Aly's sudden change, joining Lucian. Trying to kill you. It wasn't her. I suppose I'm glad she's come around, but tread lightly. She was close with Melissa. And it sounds like she's reverted to her old ways, cleaning up after other's mistakes."

Quinton danced around the details, eventually explaining Alycia's primary role had been to cover up and "extinguish" any fires that would lead back to Tempus. At any cost. "Secrecy comes at an unfortunate price. Bring her to me and pray I can clear this up with Alycia. We'll figure out what to do with Lucian." He gave directions to his room—of course, it was a penthouse in a hotel over-looking Las Vegas Boulevard.

I slinked back to the car, carrying the weight of the world into the driver's seat.

"Alright," I said, turning to her. "We're going to a friend—" I stopped, surprised to see her glaring back, burning a hole through me. "You heard everything, didn't you?"

"It was cracked," she said, pointing at the half open passenger-side window. I flashed a fake smile and shook my head. "And I am a special agent for the government, remember? You think I'm just going to twiddle my thumbs?"

So she heard everything, no strange magic protecting Tempus secrets. There was something special about her, that was for certain. A sharp pain shot through my neck and settled between my temples. The headache might have been there before, but became hard to ignore.

"I'm not the best person to answer your questions," I said while grimacing through the pain. "I'll take you to someone who can," I lied, maybe. Hopefully Quinton knew what our next step was. He was the one that called *me* into this, after all.

Guilt tugged at me harder than the seatbelt. Hitting Alycia felt horrible, even though I was certain it saved Mara's life. Could I smooth things over with her? I scrolled through the contacts on Melissa's phone and tapped Alycia's number.

"What the hell is that?" Mara exclaimed at the loud buzzing in front of her.

The ringing hummed in my ear while the buzzing continued. After a few seconds, I shook my head and ended the call with an obvious realization. "Her phone's in the glove box."

Mara exhaled relief, showing shades of embarrassment before opening the compartment. "Yup, here's a phone. And... what the—is this real?"

She held open a leather wallet. Through the clear plastic cover, I caught a picture of Alycia next to the Interpol logo.

Even after answering her question a third time, Mara remained hesitant, her face wrinkled with worry and suspicion. I put the car in drive and skidded onto the main road.

"Seriously," I said. "I haven't been on the best of terms with her either, you know. Not too long ago, she was palled up with Lucian trying to kill me." I cocked my head to her, keeping one eye on the road. "Don't forget, *you* were trying to shoot me just a few hours ago."

She grit her teeth and rocked back and forth, staring out the window. "An Interpol agent wants me dead..."

The day seemed to have finally caught up to her. No judgment—if I just escaped from a secret hideout that sank into the ground, only to be held at gunpoint by a foreign government agent—I would be frazzled. At least I would have, before learning about Tempus. Now things are a bit less shocking.

A car sped by, cutting us off without using their blinker. Mara jumped at the speeder's loud engine, tearing her from the mini crisis. "Why are you driving so slow? Hurry and let's get to this friend. I need to call my partner back. That bitch took my phone."

I couldn't help but laugh. The all-too-familiar existential dread had sunk in. "I'm already going over the speed limit. Not to mention I'm supposed to be dead, remember? We don't need any extra attention. Besides, talking to your partner should be at the bottom of your list right now. You'll only put him in danger."

She blew out a long stream of air. She was cute, in a bratty kind of way. But the connection wasn't the same. My mind wandered to Olivia. I hoped she was safe, wherever she was. Quinton was going to tell me everything. I would make sure of it.

"It's not polite to stare," Mara said with more annoyance than anger.

I wiped the stupid grin off my face. "Oh sorry, I—"

Mara yelled over the honking from the incoming car. "Hey! Eyes on the road!"

I turned the wheel sharply and merged back into the lane. "Sorry. I must have drifted off there."

"Maybe I should drive? You seem preoccupied."

"No, no. I'm good." I breathed deeply, focusing ahead. "I've got this."

Between the daydreaming and memories pulling me around, being in the present moment seemed even more difficult than usual. A marker declaring that the Vegas Strip was mere minutes away drifted by. Each second, more signs of civilization replaced the long stretches of open sand. Now nearing the nighttime, the lights from the casinos illuminated a cloudy skyline.

A ding sent my attention to the console. The car was suddenly running low on gas. Last I checked, we had well over half a tank and hadn't driven far. "I guess we need a fill-up. I think the fuel gauge is off."

Mara nodded, remaining silent until we arrived at the

gas station. "I gotta pee anyway," she said. "I'll be quick. Can you grab me a frozen coke?"

I nodded. Without eating or drinking anything for hours, refueling this body sounded good. After topping off the tank, I headed inside to pay. I wasn't too discerning about the snack purchases, trying to keep a low profile with the attendant in case I had made it to evening news.

I handed Mara a drink and protein bar, surprised by the ear to ear smile. "You seem like you're in a better mood," I said.

After a long slurp from the straw, she slinked in her seat and relaxed her shoulders. "I'm just ready to get out of this car."

I TURNED ONTO THE STRIP. Multicolored lights filled the street, blinking and flashing in every direction to create a vibrant, dazzling display. In the lane next to us, a moving billboard truck slammed on its brakes, narrowly rear ending a taxi. I slowed the car, braking for the group of pedestrians who stumbled into the street a few seconds too late.

"Watch out man!" a tourist shouted, raising his fist at the taxi before racing after his friends.

"Good thing you were paying attention," Mara said with a heavy dose of sarcasm.

I muttered a crude retort and continued. The lively energy of partygoers drifted about the strip. A glowing neon party bus buzzed across the median, the excessive bass both soothing and annoying at the same time. I eased forward, extra careful of the wandering visitors tempting the fates.

Pins and needles prickled across my skin. Overhead, the giant billboard stood tall. A reminder of the moment Hagaki's debut album cover was unveiled to the world. The advertisement forced memories of a short residency at the casino underneath. Three months of performing the same songs to tourists that may or may not have even known my stuff. But as the hottest up and comer, tickets were hard to come by. Today, instead of my intimidating stance, the sign now promoted the latest acrobatic show at the theater across the street. The small reminders of fame felt especially annoying today.

My shoulder twitched. The pulsation, not unlike a heartbeat, drew my attention to the left. Three cars behind, a navy blue van hovered above the smaller sports cars in the driver's side mirror. It looked government issue, but was too far to confirm. A soft sigh escaped my lips before I focused back on the moving traffic ahead. I snuck a glance at Mara, finding she had been stealing glances in the mirror as well. Subtle changes in her posture showed a rising excitement.

An uncomfortable tension hovered in the air. Suspicions rising, I'd go all in that we were being followed. Under other circumstances, I was in the right place to have the odds on my side. This was a bet I was hoping to lose.

She caught me watching and shot back an uneasy smile. "This traffic is something, huh?" If I wasn't listening for it, I may not have noticed the slight tremble in her voice.

So much for coincidence. She was up to something.

The visit to Quinton's penthouse would have to wait. It was too risky to chance leading anyone there. Time for a change of plans. In order not to tip off the prying agent, I'd need to fake a call from my long-lost brother and clue him in.

At the next painfully long red light, the sea of pedestrians and Mara's constant, shifting gaze became the perfect distraction. I carefully drew Melissa's cell phone from my pocket, keeping it nestled at my side near the door. Slowly scrolling the contacts one handed, I landed on Quinton's number. Just as I was ready to dial, the phone buzzed with an incoming call from the same number.

"Speak of the devil," I answered. "I was just thinking about you, *Mr. Q.*" Hopefully, the stupid greeting was enough to clue him in something was awry.

I lowered the receiver's volume and held the phone tight to the disappointment of my passenger's inquisitive glance. I shot an intimidating scowl, causing her to look away and shift uncomfortably in the leather.

"Hmm. Had a feeling I'd call?" Quinton answered over the busy ambience of a game room floor. "Sounds like you're aware our plans changed. We need to—"

"Yessir," I interrupted. "Just some light traffic is all. We are almost to you," I said in a relaxed tone, casually nodding. "We didn't expect it to be this *crowded.*"

I waited through rustling and clanking before Quinton continued. "Sorry about that. So it's a one-way line, ok. I'll text you with details. Let me know if anything changes." The call disconnected. Thankfully he honed in on my more than subtle cues.

I kept up the ruse to dead air. "Sounds good. Can't

wait to see your place. See you soon," I said to the windshield and prying ears, before putting the cellphone on my lap.

Mara squirmed, tapping on her knees and turned to face me. "Everything okay?" I wondered if she realized she was grinding her teeth, making the cutesy smile a little too exaggerated.

"Oh yeah. He probably thought I got lost or something." The lie seemed to settle her worry, sending her gaze back to the mirrors and city lights.

I muted the phone before the text came through. Our new rendezvous took us off the main strip, closer to the outskirts of Fremont Street. The traffic lightened up as we pulled further away from the more popular casinos, exposing the van even more. Now about two car lengths behind, whoever followed was doing a really shitty job of being discreet. Through the tinted windows, I caught the outline of police light bars. Standard government issue for sure. How did they find me? I was certain this was no coincidence—these guys weren't *that* good. Plus, Alycia would have checked Mara for tracking devices. Somehow, Mara must have tipped them off. That left my own ineptitude, once again putting trust in the wrong people.

As I cut the wheel in a hard turn without warning, I wondered if I would ever learn my lesson.

"What the hell!" Mara yelled while being tossed back and forth from the sharp U-turn.

Just as suspected, the dark van slammed on its brakes and attempted to change lanes. My well-timed maneuver gave the follower no option but to circle around the median and dodge the confused drivers. Even with the sudden direction change, I only gained a few seconds' distance.

Now a few blocks from old Vegas, the streets seemed strangely deserted, a stark contrast to the bustling city in the rear-view. Putting the old car's acceleration to the test, we zipped by small ranch-style houses, aging apartments, and an occasional off-strip museum. A looming mountain only heightened the disparity, signaling that we had entered another world—metaphorically speaking.

Mara gained her breath, pulling up from the armrest into an alert posture. "What the fuck are you doing?"

Well over thirty miles above the speed limit, I raced between a sparse smattering of cars on the four-lane road. Behind, the dark outline of our follower took shape, still blocks away.

"I told you to leave them out of this!" I said, easing off the gas to make a quick left turn.

A single blue light flashed in the distance, handling the curve surprisingly smoother than the old Thunderbird. I had the speed and size advantage, but outmaneuvering looked out of the question. This would call for something drastic. A busy intersection quickly approached. And with it, dozens of law-abiding drivers waited their turn for the red light to change while other vehicles zipped across.

"Are you fucking serious? You're going to kill us!" Mara tightened her seat belt and looked out at the road, her serious expression suggesting she was calculating her odds of survival.

I've done some pretty stupid things behind the wheel. Like when I intentionally brake checked a sports car at high speed. But playing Frogger through a busy crossroad was taking it to a new extreme. I hoped shock and fear would prevent Mara from trying to take the wheel. Her darting eyes telegraphed the thought.

"Don't even think about it," I said, pulling into the opposing traffic lane. Thankfully, it was clear—for the time being.

The van merged over to join us on the wrong side of the road but slowed the closer we got to the intersection. Now seconds away, I focused on the blur of cars flying across in front of us, attempting to time the crossing. As if by miracle, the opposing traffic began to slow—a combination of their light turning yellow and spotting the incoming chase. Or pure luck.

Narrowly dodging a car in the first lane through, we slipped across the intersection nearly unscathed—physically, at least. As we crossed into the open road ahead, a blue sports car zipped by in the last lane, hoping to run its own red light. It gently clipped our bumper, sending us skidding off balance. The Ferrari wasn't so lucky. The *gentle* graze sent it spinning out of control, its rear wheel slamming into a light post. Luckily, it was a one car crash —hopefully with no casualties.

The rearview showed the van blocked by a mess of cars. Good. It would take a while for the road to clear while they figured out what to do. Quinton's new meeting spot was just a few miles away—a museum dedicated to old Vegas.

Mara rubbed her trembling hands against bouncing legs, an attempt to soothe racked nerves. "I... just." She exhaled hard and regained composure, showing the ferocity from earlier today. "I needed backup. I don't exactly trust you. Even if you're not a terrorist, you already destroyed a warehouse with the woman who almost killed—"

She didn't have a chance to finish. A jarring clash accompanied a loud thump from behind. I looked away for seconds, apparently long enough for the shiny silver coupe to join in. Even less discrete than their friend, the push bar and police lights unmistakably identified them as the law. The lack of siren and lights meant they were less interested in pulling me over and more focused on getting me off the road.

Mara's head rapidly swayed, checking each mirror. "He was only supposed to follow!"

The coupe pulled back to speed around, racing parallel to my passenger side. Thankfully, the stretch of road appeared relatively clear, giving us ample space to race well over sixty miles per hour. Mara threw her hands up and shrugged at the other driver—the pale man I had the displeasure of meeting earlier.

"You're not making this easy." I scanned the rearview to see it was empty and decided to warn her, "hold on."

With a better feel for the car's handling, I braked and turned, sending us into as close to a one-eighty as possible. The coupe took several seconds to react to the direction change. I took advantage of the lead and swerved into an alleyway. Every second mattered. A few more of those and maybe I had a chance of escaping, especially as there weren't any others joining in the chase. At least yet.

Another abrupt turn put us back on a desolate stretch of road, surrounded by empty warehouses and closed businesses. I opened the window to let a waft of cool night air flow in, the spicy aroma of sagebrush met with a less pleasant urban smell causing me to cringe.

A yellow street light appeared overhead. My foot instinctively pushed the gas to roar faster through the empty intersection. Almost empty. As we passed through, a black SUV sat waiting at the light—Alycia's squinted eyes peering back at me from the driver's seat.

Not waiting for a green light, the SUV shot forward. Wheels squealed to announce the new pursuit, leaving a plume of dirty smoke in their wake. I just couldn't catch a break today. I added pressure on the gas, hoping to keep the lead. A quick glance showed my luck was running low. The SUV barreled forward, no regard for its surroundings. "Sit tight we've—"

Conversation was clearly not on the table right now. Several quick crackles erupted from behind, taking us both by surprise. I briefly lost control of the car, swerving from lane to lane before stabilizing the wheel. In the rearview, cracks spidered out from three quarter-sized holes.

Mara slouched further after reaching to her waist, instinctually for the gun she was stripped of earlier. She popped her head back up, studying the window before sliding down again. "Bulletproof, for now at least," she said.

I pushed harder on the pedal, jolting my passenger forward. Her hand caught the dashboard, bracing the impact. Her knuckles gripped tight, ready for more erratic driving. And for good reason. I took another hard turn, wheels fighting to grab hold of the concrete underneath. The car slid further than I hoped, just barely missing a row of old newspaper vending machines.

I regained traction and scanned the rear. The SUV fell back, passed by the silver coupe. Both struggled, skidding through the turn. I let out a faint chuckle.

"What's so damn funny!" Mara stammered.

"This just feels way too familiar." I dodged a few slow moving cars and blasted through an empty intersection. "You know, you'd already be safe if you just listened."

"None of that matters if we're—"

The back window exploded sending glass ricocheting inside. Small fragments scattered and bounced into the center console. A sharp edge grazed my arm, opening a small trickle of blood streaming near my elbow.

From my driver's side mirror, I caught Alycia retracting her pistol. She kept her promise.

Both seconds behind, our pursuers raced parallel to each other. The churning in my stomach was justified.

Mara's partner didn't take kindly to the gunfire and changed targets, ramming into the side of the SUV.

"Call him off! She'll kill him! We can't drag anyone into this!" I yelled.

Mara's jaw dropped, watching the two followers swerving and darting across the lanes. Engrossed in a dangerous game of chicken, the vehicles dodged one another while struggling to keep up with my own frantic driving.

I added more intensity to my voice while the battle followed. "I know you tipped him off! Tell him to back off!"

Mara relaxed her tightly wound fists, aggressively popping the glove compartment open. She retrieved Alycia's cell phone and dialed. Of course. If I had a free hand, I'd slap myself. She must have called Blake while I got her snacks. Last nice thing I do.

"Blake! It's me, fall back!" she yelled into the phone, an eye still on the action close behind. "I'm OK, trust me. Fall back now and stay safe. I'll call later." I couldn't hear a response but from the context, her partner apprehensively agreed.

Before another sharp turn, I realized the impromptu battle had given us a significant lead. In the distance, I watched as Blake gave the SUV one last well placed slam, sending the larger vehicle off balance into a parked pickup truck. The coupe turned in another direction and disappeared while the SUV pulled back from the truck then quickly lost speed. Before it came to a stop, a hubcap rolled into the street from a shaky front tire.

Mara closed her eyes and nodded with a sigh of relief. One I finally felt comfortable sharing.

Now certain we weren't followed, I pulled the car behind an alleyway near the Old Vegas Graveyard. The front of the several acre outdoor museum sported a worn admission sign touting a spectacular tour of the past. Fifteen dollars, ten on Tuesday.

A few more steps revealed a tiny sun-faded message stuck to the glass double doors of the giftshop: *Thanks for the Memories.* Several neon signs peaked over the chain-link fence. Faintly in the darkness, I clocked several relics of days past. Pieces of a pirate ship sat next to giant light bulb covered letters, the kind I remembered from old gangster documentaries about Vegas. With only a baby floodlight illuminating the walkway, the entrance was barely visible. Moonlight and the distant casinos struggled to help, wrapping the old building in an eerie glow from above.

"You sure this is safe?" Mara said, a hand still hovering near her outer thigh despite being unarmed.

"Safer than the road." I shot her a smile and continued up the cracked walkway, following the graffiti-enhanced arrows behind the giftshop. She made sure to check each dark nook, taking time to remind me of our ambush risks after I rolled my eyes. As she peered behind a malfunctioning vending machine, I suddenly realized the absence of nausea and prickly sensations. Earlier today, just being near her made me sick to my stomach. Maybe the change had something to do with our close proximity over the past hour. Another question for Vance, if we could find the tracker.

The area itself seemed to radiate a biting cold. Thankfully, the wind had died down making the desert night tolerable. Hints of mint and tobacco lingered in the air as we traipsed past the fence.

The gravel crunched under our feet, both on guard, scanning between every neon sign and dark corner. I felt a sense of awe surrounded by the rows of casino history. Unfortunately, the place had seen better days. Even in the dirt, an assortment of weeds found their way to the surface, hoping to find life in any place they could. Most of the signs had missing bulbs—colorful pieces scattered along the dirt pathway. I imagined the disappointment of whoever was once the warden of the museum.

"This must have been a pretty cool place," I said quietly, vacillating between childlike awe and the need to defend myself at a moment's notice.

"It was." A light flashed from the darkness drawing our eyes between a giant cartoony skull and an equally exaggerated oversized slot machine. The minty herb aroma returned, wafting from the embers of Quinton's cigar. "The owner died last year in a car accident. His partner couldn't bear to keep it open."

Quinton sauntered out from between the signs. He carried himself with a swagger, showing no signs of our frantic conversation earlier. His elegant long grey peacoat covered an expensive looking collared shirt and black tie. Either the temperature suddenly dipped or his appearance had a cryptic effect. I shivered as goosebumps ran up my forearms, and from Mara hugging herself close, she felt the same. Her eyes studied the silver-haired man while taking a step back, turning me into a barrier between them.

"You remember your friend AJ, right?" he said, taking a puff from the cigar. A plume of smoke made it look almost appetizing, despite my distaste for gross, overproduced modern tobacco—no comparison to authentic Chinese herbs from centuries ago.

"The owner, Danny, was a good friend of his," Quinton continued, pausing to watch my reaction.

I hadn't thought of AJ in months. One of my celebrity hip-hop friends from the future. Well, *a future.* One that no longer exists after I traveled back. I visited him last year, but it was such a short exchange. Hell, he didn't even know who I was. But I had to give him a warning, even if in passing: *"Don't take a deal with Paradise Records."* The record label whose president would eventually kill him, then me—all triggering this whole time traveling mess.

It seemed like the right thing to do—and I was still here, so I must have avoided creating a paradox. My mind started its trek down the all too familiar rabbit hole before stopping. *Time travel is not like the movies,* I reminded myself. Man, life was so much simpler before Tempus came around. Dealing with the reincarnation thing was enough on its own.

The silence, along with his grin, gave the impression he took delight in the question, watching the puzzled look on my face. "Sad story. Danny was on his way to work when a semi-truck lost control. Horrible accident." Quinton punctuated each sentence with a quick puff and too much silence for my liking. I sensed he had a point and let him dance through the monologue. "Danny *would have* been attending AJ's first local show. A try-out of sorts. For Paradise Records."

My heart sank. My neck drifted to the ground while I closed my eyes and inhaled the mix of fresh and minty air. Dirt rustled from behind, followed by a hand on my shoulder.

"Hey, you okay?" Mara whispered.

I straightened my posture and nodded. Angry at Quinton for his terrible delivery. Angry at myself for the ripple I'd caused. The lives I changed.

Quinton tapped the cigar, causing a shower of ash to dance in the breeze before delicately placing it on the aged gold and black circus-themed sign. "Every action has a reaction, Jay. This is a hard lesson. You need to stick to the script. I hope this drives the point home." He stepped closer, his dress shoes even sounding elegant on the dirt. "I've made sure AJ is back on track. And you're looking at the new owner of this place. The soft reopening is scheduled in two months. Tempus exists for a reason, after all."

Mara nestled in closer from behind as Quinton glided forward, stopping uncomfortably close. Her warm cherry chapstick breath tickled the back of neck. An extreme contrast to the minty sharp words of the man glaring ahead. But he wasn't wrong. My actions came at a sickly cost. Save a life, end another—or worse. But with what happened today, was this really the time to dig up some-thing from over a year ago?

"Forgive my manners." Quinton shifted his position and raised his hand toward Mara. I instinctively moved over, shielding her from his reach prompting disappoint-ment in his eyes. The expression morphed to a knowing smile, nodding as he stepped back.

"You'll have to forgive me, Q." I added an emphasis on the nickname, hoping to remind him of Melissa and the nightmare we had just come from. All the emotion I'd stored up today came spilling out. "I get it. I fucked up, and I keep fucking up. Lesson learned. You could have told me last year, you know. Weren't you supposed to be my guide? Or did you forget that little ceremony of weirdos in the cemetery?"

The smile disappeared. His gaze drifted to Mara and then off into the distance. "You're right. Not to offload the blame, but I hope you understand. I was instructed to leave you be. In fact, I was explicitly ordered to stay away. Provide money and a home. Ensure you were playing your music at the bar. And nothing else until further notice." He looked to the ground and cupped one of his wrists, wringing it gently like you would tend to a sprain. "I'm guilty of breaking the rules myself. I discreetly checked on you from time to time. Made sure you were safe." His cheeks developed a hint of red. Was he embarrassed?

Mara stepped into the foreground to meet my side. "Okay. Nice family reunion and all, but it's fucking cold out here and I don't understand why you're dragging me into this. Where is Lucian and who's the British bitch that almost killed me?"

Quinton chuckled. "I apologize. It's much easier to avoid the elephant in the room. Nevertheless, it's still here." He turned and motioned for us to follow.

He led in silence, walking us through the darkened outdoor museum toward the main office. More of old Vegas flanked us. Neatly arranged signs of all shapes and sizes led us through the winding maze. Some of the outdoor decor dated back to the fifties, several as recent as the nineties. I recognized the worn genie's lamp and oversized cowboy hat neons from movies released decades ago.

The white stone office doubled as a gift shop, comparatively boring to the history outside. Quinton held the rusty door open for us. *Such a gentleman.* "Come on in. Lights on the left."

I took the lead and crept into the dark building, only traces of the moon and outdoor light shining through. Finding the light was easier said than done. I felt along the wall, blindly searching until the sharp metal of a switch nipped my finger. "Ow!" I belted before tapping on the lights and kissing my finger like a baby. I realized my child-like reaction and shrugged with a smile to Mara. She wasn't too concerned—her jaw slightly agape, wide eyes looking past me with awe.

"What the hell is this?" Mara said, walking past me while surveying the poorly lit office.

I quit sucking my finger and joined in her looks of wonder. The black acoustic tiled ceiling and walls accented the deep black and gray marble floor. In front of the dark walls, rows of monitors began flashing to life, some showing a variety of live camera footage. Others displayed detailed, colorful charts and diagrams filled with strange looking symbols. A few of them were reminiscent of what Melissa had been watching earlier in the day. The room smelled of new electronics: a comforting combo of steel and plastic swirled together. A small desk sat in the corner accompanied by a leather office chair, both next to a haphazard pile of discarded styrofoam and open monitor boxes.

A soft click snapped behind as Quinton walked past us. "I apologize for the mess. It was a temporary spot I never ended up using. I'm going to clear this all out soon." He waved a hand for us to follow him into a smaller room containing the same dark decor with less distractions on the wall. Two leather sofas faced each other with a black coffee table in between. In the corner, a dark brown, worn-oak cabinet stood looking out of place with the rest of the aesthetic. "Have a seat."

Mara shot me a look of confusion, my only reply a shrug and a hand for her to sit first. She plopped onto the couch, then stretched out her legs while sinking her head against the cushion until facing the ceiling. I settled in next to her, finding it was more comfortable than it looked. We both sat in silence, breathing in the warm indoor air.

A dull clunk against the table had us sitting upright, brought back to the present to see Quinton setting out glasses. He poured us water from a crystal jug then reclined into the opposing couch. Having shed the peacoat, I could see his black suit coat and dress pants, both having a slight purple sheen depending on how he shifted in the light. He pulled at his necktie, loosening it then setting it on the couch beside him.

"It's been quite a day, hasn't it?" He swiped several loose gray hairs from his face, his demeanor taking a sudden shift from formal to casual.

I shot an annoyed glance at Mara, hoping to find camaraderie with the stranger who didn't fully trust me. To be fair, I didn't trust her either.

"Mara, how much information has Jay provided?" Quinton took a sip from his glass, then ran a palm over his beard clearing any excess water.

A snort escaped Mara's nose. "Let's see. *I need to take you to my friend.* That's about the gist of it." She grabbed a glass, finishing the water in seconds before setting it on the table with a loud clunk. "Oh, and by the way. You're all impeding an active federal investigation. So it would be in your best interests to start talking." Her gaze danced between me and Quinton. "I'll ask again. Who was the woman that tried to kill me? And what do you know of Lucian and his dealings in the Middle East?"

Quinton ran a hand through his beard again and looked up to the ceiling for a moment. "Let's see. Where shall I begin?"

I LEANED back in the leather chair, staring at the monitors. What was I looking at? Most of the screens appeared to display financial transactions from banks across the world. The others scrolled through news reports and camera footage from outdoor areas. Los Angeles, Cairo, London, even a few here in Vegas. Every few minutes, I snuck a look at the open office door. Mara's posture shifted drastically at each glance. Right now, she was leaning forward and appeared to hang off whatever Quinton was saying. I wanted to stay in the room and listen—hopes of learning any nuggets of info to fulfill my own curiosities. But I was my own worst enemy: after interjecting and talking over them for the third time, both Quinton and Mara *politely* suggested I step out.

Over the soothing hum of electronics, I heard the word *Tempus*, followed by names of the various players from today. All with no issues—like Quinton's throat closing or Mara's ears hissing from a mysterious force. I chuckled, remembering Blake's sad attempt at an interrogation. Quinton took notice and closed the door, limiting my eavesdropping to a muffled conversation.

I hopped from the chair and wandered over. Just as I was about to cup my hand against the wood to listen in, a light glow filled the room from outside. Now in front of the boarded-up windows, I peeked through a small opening to see most of the signs were lit. Neons tubes spewed vibrant, sparkling color across the fenced-in field. I'd hate to see their electric bill. My eyes shifted to a small flashing replica of the Statue of Liberty. I squinted, gazing at Lady Liberty when suddenly life became a blur of hazy gold. Century-old thoughts raced back, lost in a visit to the real deal.

A loud click echoed from the office, piquing my curiosity even more and possibly preventing a new unlocking of distant memories. My eyes narrowed on the closed door. The curiosity won. I darted across the room and pulled the door open, startling Mara, midway into removing her shirt over her head. She finished, set the shirt on the cushion beside her, and crossed her arms over a black sports bra. Other than the initial shock, she was indifferent as I loomed from the doorway.

Quinton stood before the old cabinet holding a shiny silver device. My mind shot to the first time seeing it. *"Don't let them scan you."* Quinton's words echoed in my brain—his warning before I met Pharaoh and Alycia. A warning before their attempt to skirt the Tempus customs so I'd join Lotus without the pomp and circumstance of an official ceremony. A big no-no in the secret world of Tempus.

Quinton's face leered back with annoyance. "It won't hurt," he reassured her. Quinton looked back up at me. "If you'll just give us a minute, please."

My heartbeat grew faster, my past traumas clawing back to haunt me. Why was he breaking the rules he had been so dead set on following? I stepped closer, noticing the barcode-like tattoo on Mara's shoulder. It gave off an eerie lilac glow, especially pronounced on her smooth sepia skin. I froze, reliving the first time I realized I was branded with the symbols—imagining what the woman must be thinking.

She hesitated, studying the mark the best she could from its position on her back. Quinton gave her an abridged explanation, confirming what I already knew. How the mark glowed various colors depending on the proximity of Tempus members. He left out the part about how it also changed if you were being tracked. I briefly wondered where Vance was, hoping he was alive. If I had a to-do list, finding him would be somewhere near the top.

"What are you doing?" I said, blending the question into a statement.

"Scanning her in." He stepped back and relaxed his posture. "Oh." His expression changed, reading the fear and anger on my face. "Things are... different now."

"No creepy secret Tempus council meeting? You're saying the world won't end because of infighting from not letting her choose an alignment? What if she doesn't want Lotus, what about Orchid and the other groups I don't even know of? Yeah, it's time for some answers." Heat washed over my face.

Mara relaxed her body and lowered her hands, turning with shock of embarrassment. The expression faded, returning to the confidence from before. "Wait, so you're saying I'm not supposed to do this?" She looked back and forth between our faces with annoyance on her own.

Quinton set the device down and held his hands high,

pleading for peace. "Jay. I would love to tell you I have all the answers. Please trust me in that this is the right thing to do."

I leaned against the doorframe and relaxed my jaw after realizing I was clenching my teeth. "How do you know?"

He shrugged, almost playfully. "With Pharaoh gone, I'm in charge."

"Of Lotus?"

The smile wasn't one of joy. In fact, he looked to be masking a migraine. "Do you recall meeting One?"

I nodded. One—the cryptic name of the equally mysterious robed leader who swore me in to Tempus last year. I had chosen neutrality instead of joining Orchid, Lotus, or any of the other branches. *Or threads*—it was hard keeping track of the lingo for a group that left me spinning in the wind for months. I'd learned more about their inner workings today than in the last year.

"Jay, shortly after that meeting, One disappeared. The trial deciding the fates of Lucian and Alycia never occurred as promised. They remained frozen, exiled in stasis. With Orchid's leader and Lotus's second in command gone, Pharaoh called an emergency meeting." I scoffed, partly out of jealousy. He read my mind. "Yes, you were left out intentionally. Again, by design, orders from above. But I also watched as you pieced together a normal life. I saw glimmers of joy breaking through. Something I didn't wish to muddy with Tempus affairs."

I felt a lump in my throat. Another reminder he really cared. Probably a good thing to have a break from the time traveling drama, even if for a few months.

"After a careful deliberation, the sects were disbanded." He paused, opening his palm toward me. "In a way, through your actions you unified us."

Not bad for having no idea what I was doing. I embraced the sense of redemption, especially after my little seven year excursion was once heralded as the end of civilization. At least by a few members of the secret group.

"So, no more underground council meetings?" I asked.

He nodded and picked up the device, then kneeled next to Mara. With an eased posture, she pointed her tattooed shoulder toward him.

"Wait!" I said, stepping forward. "Aren't you forgetting something? I know I'm not usually the voice of reason, but remember what Melissa said earlier? I believe she used the word *disastrous*. Something about *treading lightly*." I realized I was waving my hands as I spoke and held them steady. "We're supposed to join Tempus *after* we cheat death, right?" I had figured out that much. We die and reset a bit of time. *Unless you're me.* "We've been stuck in this loop, meaning she's cheated death dozens of times. What if we've already done this before? Or if you scan her and, I don't know, it tears open the timeline and causes a black hole? You weren't at the station earlier, things got *weird*." My fears may have been irrational, although my gut thought otherwise, imagining the epicenter Alycia spoke of. Maybe I should skip the late night sci-fi movies.

"Woah, woah." Mara reached for her shirt and covered her chest. "You never said anything about dying. And black holes? What the fuck!"

Quinton sat back, looking up at me from the ground.

His expression showed no sign of acknowledging the end of the universe. "You're a quick study. Cheating death, well, something like that. That's the working theory. Death or near death causes us to shift back." He smiled, looking back at Mara. "That loop you spoke of, the dream of dying and waking. It's true. It's unlike anything we've heard of."

"So what happens if you scan me and you're not supposed to?" Mara said.

I heard the duffle bag plop down near me before I saw it. "She could bleed out from her eyes and ears until she dies in excruciating pain. Or she becomes one of us," Alycia's sharp British accent commanded from behind.

"Ever the optimist, Aly," Quinton said, setting the device down again and standing to face our new guest.

Alycia brushed into my arm as she walked by, turning with narrowed eyes and a mischievous smile. "I can't believe you took the Thunderbird," she said in a low, breathy voice. "You owe me for the window."

I did my best to hide the shock from her sudden appearance. "You shot it!"

Alycia smirked and sat on the couch opposite Mara—who showed no hints of surprise—expecting her captor's return. What the hell happened behind that closed door? I looked back to Alycia. She found a change of clothes—now dressed in form fitting black leggings and a zipped up black leather cycling jacket. Her red lips matched the bands holding her hair up in a tight bun. She looked stunning. Different from the woman I had been tagging along with, but I'll admit she was gorgeous in the greasy mechanic outfit, too. I wondered where she had the time to change. She turned to me, cocking her head with wide eyes.

"Hagaki? Jay?" Quinton said from the other end of the room.

My face got flush. Did I just get caught staring? "I must have... unlocked, a memory?" I lied, complete with stutter.

Alycia shook her head. "*Sure*", I could almost hear her saying with her eyes before looking back at Mara.

The agent crossed her arms, now dressed in her shirt and jacket, tapping her foot in a nervous rhythm. Her eyes met Alycia's. I watched as their faces went through a number of expressions—from fear to anger to confusion and finally an apprehensive acceptance.

Alycia broke the silence, kicking her feet up on the table. "I guess I owe you an apology." Either her words were extra proper, or she was pushing her British accent on purpose. "With me out of commission, I haven't been able to play middleman with the feds." She looked over at me for a moment before continuing, suggesting I had been responsible for turning her into a statue the past year. "And I must be rusty." Her eyes locked on Mara. "I can normally detect other travelers. You're... different."

Mara dropped her hands and ran them up and down her thighs. "So, what's this about dying? Could the scanning really kill me?"

"Alycia can't help herself," Quinton said with no hint of humor. "She's right though, you are different." He looked around the room to Alycia and me, then back to Mara. "We all feel it. Something I haven't sensed before."

"So you scan me, and then what?"

"I believe it will stop the loop, at least," Quinton said.

"Wait," I interjected. "Believe? This was your grand plan and you don't even know if it will work?" I was getting red for a different reason now. "You've already lied to me once. Remember what you said in the cemetery before that ceremony? *We travel in pairs,*" I said in a mocking tone. "I remember everything now, *brother.*" I looked over to Alycia, imagining her as Sofie for the first time despite the countless visions. "There's more to the story than you're telling me."

Alycia remained relaxed on the couch, a smug amusement on her face. "I'm not sure where I fit in any of this, but someone has to pay for what they did to Melissa."

"Enough," Quinton raised his voice for the first time, commanding our attention. "Yes, I left some details out. I thought I was protecting you but I see that's not the case. There's still so much none of us know. Even me, now at the top. What I do know is that we need to acclimate Mara and bring Lucian to justice." Mara flinched at the word *acclimate* but remained silent.

"I'll drink to that." Alycia raised a glass of water as a toast, then took a swig. "Never liked the fool, but he had a compelling argument." I avoided eye contact, guessing she was staring daggers through me.

"Not so fast, Alycia," I stated matter-of-factly. "You owe me answers, Quinton. Where is Olivia and why have you been lying to me? Tell me everything. You're in charge now, no excuses."

Quinton inhaled deeply and stroked his beard, appearing deep in thought.

Silence.

Alycia stood from the couch and rolled her eyes. "Okay. Since he won't, I'll tell you." She looked between me and Mara as she spoke. "Some of us are born with what we call Hx Cells. They give us abilities. Traveling back, tracking, and for others, increasing insight in shifts of the timeline."

Mara and I must have shared the same expression—something in the room smelled rank. It sounded like something out of a bad sci-fi movie. Well, maybe a decent one with some plot holes and a lot of hype to live up to.

"Alycia!" Quinton shouted from the corner, picking the device up for a third time. "How can you even say that with a straight face?"

"Hey," she replied casually, waving him off with her hand. "You try being in a lucid coma for a year. At least give me a laugh. I'm tired of all this running around. The secrecy too." She turned to face me, catching me rubbing my forehead in exhaustion. She traded the playful posture for a rigid stiffness. "Why don't you tell us, Mr. Seven Years?"

Quinton forced us out of the room, slamming the door hard, almost hitting Alycia. Scolding us like children for misbehaving, we both burst out laughing at the absurdity of the situation. To be fair, we *were* a distraction, although I didn't think the barbs we traded were "flirting".

The room of flashing screens was eerily quiet. After a minute of awkward silence, we went outside to join the circus of twinkling lights.

"I truly was going to kill that woman," Alycia said, now leaning against the brick wall with one foot back to prop herself up. She looked straight ahead at the sea of steel and brilliant color. "Part of me knew she didn't kill Melissa. But I didn't care. She knew too much." She looked over to find me, arms crossed and gazing into the electric graveyard. "Doing the right thing doesn't always feel right."

I let out a nervous chuckle and put a foot of my own on the railing in front of the wall. "You're the Tempus assassin, I get it." At least I thought I did.

"It's not just that, though. Part of me enjoyed hurting her." She exhaled, sending wisps of her chilly breath in my direction. I caught a whiff of peppermint. "I don't think that's me."

"I know it's not," I said with confidence, imagining Sofie.

I turned to see her face contorted in confusion. "I saw your files on Hales, remember?" I explained.

She pushed herself off the wall and planted the relaxed foot on the cement. "And? It's not nice to snoop. You never finished your monologue before you knocked me out. Got some bollocks on you." With a half smile, she walked closer, both of us looking out at the lights. "It's you, isn't it?" There was a hint of surprise in the question.

I shrugged, the motion small enough she might not have noticed.

"Hmmph." She turned and hopped up on the railing, swinging her feet playfully. She appeared celestial, halos dazzling above from old Vegas. "Makes sense now why Quinton was so obsessed with finding you. And—" Her feet stopped swinging and she turned to face me. The pallor across her face was striking. She gripped the railing hard, knuckles turning a sickly white. "Melissa. God. She was a message for you." Her head sank, a big chunk of hair breaking loose from the bun.

I couldn't deny I had the same thought. Her throat, like a cut from The Butcher, this time from Lucian no doubt. "If it makes it any better, I only found out about Hales today." Silence. Her eyes remained locked on the ground under her. I turned and hopped on the railing next to her. "She meant a lot to you, didn't she?"

"She did. Not in this life, but before. I learned who she was around the time you arrived last year. I never had a chance to tell her." Her voice was filled with pain. "I wonder if she knew..."

We listened to the wind whistle through the metal of years gone by, sitting on the cold steel bars a foot apart. The internal struggle to stay quiet lost. "Do you ever question why we keep the memories of our past lives? Why we only remember certain pieces?" I chuckled and kept the questions coming like I'd opened a faucet of wonder. "Why we mess with time?"

After a quick snort of laughter, a flicker of life and color returned to her. "I used to. All of us have had the same questions at one point. It's only human to want answers." She stopped, curling her lips upward. "And I'm pretty sure we're human." Her head lifted slowly, hesitating before turning to face me. "You want to understand, I get it. Something to make sense of this. Something to give it a purpose."

She paused, staring at the brick wall in front of us, watching the reflection of the lights from behind. Stillness—broken by her laughter—a genuine giggle for the first time since leaving the room.

"What's so funny?" I asked.

"Oh, I was just thinking of when Quinton brought you to meet us for the first time." It was a strange reminder—once running for my life, now sitting next to her on a steel guard rail pondering life's mysteries. "I had to hold back from killing you there and then. And Pharaoh, with his paltry explanation of Tempus. *Gifts from the Gods*, he would say. Bloody hell, better than Lucian calling it *Magic,* or the other absurd explanations thrown about."

"So, which is it?

"I've got bad news for you. There's no elaborate answer to why. Maybe I'm too jaded, but I'll give you what the others didn't, the truth. At least my truth. It sounds that you've learned as much as us. We've simply added layers and layers of human bullshit as an attempt to make sense of it. These memories of our past seem to unlock *coincidentally* at important moments, never too early. Sometimes too late..." She drifted away for a beat. I imagined her thinking of Melissa. "As you surmised, it begins after a brush with death. Then we all go back for a ride. *Usually* a day or a week at most—and only us travelers are aware of it. At least in some way. The rest of the world goes on, thanks to us. Filling the blanks when needed."

"Like what happened a few months back? And with Mara?" I asked, appreciating her not mentioning *seven years*, her easy go-to jab.

"Yeah," she nodded. "We adjust... correct things if we need to—hence the tracking. And secrecy. And killing." The sentence was punctuated with a sigh.

I recoiled, processing a mental spike of discomfort before bringing it up—but I needed to find out. "Killing... why can't we kill each other? How does that even work?"

"More questions without good answers. Generally speaking, we can't kill each other once we're scanned, although we are not strangers to pain. And as you've experienced with your stunts today, that extends to self-inflicted injury as well." She swayed her legs playfully again before continuing. "As your resident Tempus assassin however, I have... eliminated threats. Permanently. Both internal and civilian."

"Last year, Quinton said lethal force is allowed to protect council secrecy or the *stability of the timeline.*" I used air quotes on the last part and lost balance on the railing, quickly gripping onto the bars with embarrassment. "Ahem... that seems a little vague though. Is that what happened today?"

"That's what we say. But in fact," she stopped to look around the empty outdoor museum, "It's only half the truth."

"What do you mean?"

"The injuries... the death I cause. I could end you right now, no special Tempus stipulation." The smile faded to an expression bathed in regret. "They built that logic, *those rules,* around me. Well, me and a select few that came before. I'm the only one left. And I was instructed not to reveal this to anyone." She stopped, facing me with a softness in her eyes. "The ruse is easy to keep up. I'm the only member that gets official *authorization* in the rare times we need an elimination. And I've been careful to only attack when they tell me, as you said, to protect the council, the timeline. Well, as far as they know."

So that Tempus rule was bogus, not applying to me or any of the others. Just Alycia doing their bidding when need be.

We traded a long series of expressions. Although wordless, absent of any body language, our conversation ended with her final statement, *Don't ask.* But the need to know was eating at me. I'd try again later.

I ignored the fluttering in my chest and changed the subject. "What about the scanning? The ceremonies?"

"A system to keep order, evolved over time. Some of us remember more than one life." She paused and gestured to me. "It's what has kept us threaded through the generations, so that we don't forget our function, as a whole. Many of us only remember bits, pieces of the last. You're not like most." She sucked air through her teeth while looking back to the building. "Quinton caught me up to speed on the way over."

That must have been one hell of a conversation. And Mara must have been part of it, or at least heard enough to not attack Alycia on sight. The guy must have a gift with words—convincing her from shooting out my window an hour ago to the point she's strolling in with jokes.

"Wonder what the woman knows?" she said. "Too bad we don't choose what we remember."

Her explanation was businesslike yet casual, vague yet detailing so much of what I wanted to know.

"So it's all just a made up circus," I said quietly.

"Layers of human bullshit," she repeated. "But the gifts, the magic, whatever you call it. It's real. We change the secret, candy coated shell every hundred years. Collectively piecing together our spotty memories to fill in the blanks. It's difficult to know what's real at this point —the world's longest game of telephone."

I hopped off the guard rail and took a few steps away to face her, finally ready for the burning question. "What do you know about Olivia?"

Her stoic expression changed, squinting before cocking her head to the side, still reading my face. Did I read a tinge of disappointment? "The girl you were with?"

I hoped I could jog her memory from the events of last year. "Back at the cemetery. And the hotel. She left with a man after the ceremony. Quinton called him an *original*. And he's been stringing me along, in the dark ever since." My temperature rose as the words spilled out.

Alycia dropped off the guardrail and used it to rest her back. "She's important to you?" I nodded, causing her to shift her weight onto the other side. "I had a memory come back, unlock, immediately before Quinton called me here." I started to question how he reached her without a phone—reminding myself to shut up and listen. Her words were carefully laced with long, thoughtful pauses. "From the future you took away... you were injured. Shot from the looks of it. The woman, Olivia—she was tending to you. Quinton was there, trying to stop me." She looked away, back to the flickering lights of history brightly illuminating the night sky.

Despite the sudden warmth, I felt another wave of ice flow through my veins. I walked to her side and put a hand softly on her shoulder. She recoiled as if a bee had stung her and stepped away.

After clearing her throat and another deep breath, she continued. "I killed her, Jay. I wish I knew why. I killed her. And then the dream, the memory ends."

Even though I had prepared, the words stung more than any insect. Despite that future no longer existing, my body still understood the pain. I fought the emotion and channeled the remaining parts of logic still active within. Pressing on for information, I repressed anger, grief, and a strange urge to console her.

I stuttered and stumbled over the response. "That's all you remember?"

"I wish I knew why," she repeated in a breathy tone, her eyes appearing more glassy—if she saw me, her detached stare didn't let it show.

I could feel her slipping away as the memories consumed her. Reasserting myself, I continued with a clear and direct tone. "You said the memories happened *coincidentally*." I used her words, hoping to pull her out of the daydream. "It must mean something. Just like all my memories of Whitechapel coming back today. Why now?"

The mention of *Whitechapel* jerked her back to reality with a quizzical look. "I think there was more after the memory, but it's still a haze. Something about that woman—"

Quinton's words caught us off guard from behind, "She's a traveler, like us."

If my jaw wasn't on the floor, it sure was agape. So I hadn't dragged Olivia into this? After all the long guilt-stricken nights—she was actually part of the strange illuminati time group.

I scratched my scalp too hard, almost drawing blood. "What?" is all I could muster.

Quinton joined us outside, followed by Mara close behind. She carried the confidence I remembered from the forest with a new glow radiating around her. The older man searched his long coat and pulled out a torn pack of cigarettes, crumpling it to peek inside. A throaty grunt followed the disappointment. After scanning the area with no trash in sight, the crushed mess went back into his pocket.

"You haven't had the dreams, then?" he said, folding his arms with a smug look on his face. "Well, I suppose I promised to tell you."

Alycia took a step forward and nodded to Quinton. "You tried to stop me."

"Almost did, from what I remember." A brief look of disappointment washed over before he shook it off. "After you arrived," he pointed to the British assassin. "You shot Olivia. And that's when *my* memory ends."

A fog in my soul began to lift. Etched in my brain—
the conversation from last year: Olivia's *dream* that made
no sense, not fitting with the already strange timeline.
Her memory of nursing me back to health after being
shot by my producer. How was it possible? Her story
countered my recollection: Terrance's fatal gunshot,
ending my celebrity life, killing me and sending me back,
years before I was famous.

And then it hit me. Literally. I nearly fell over as my
knees buckled under an invisible pressure. Thankfully
the guardrail was close enough to brace. Despite all three
heads turning, none raced to help. Jerks.

"You okay?" Mara said, showing hints of concern, the
most out of the group.

"She traveled first," I said at a measured pace, still
processing as I spoke. Olivia's words rang through my
head for the hundredth time: "*Another chance... I think I
tried to fix it... I tried to warn you.*" I looked at Alycia with a
painful squint. "You killed Olivia. You sent us back."

"It took you a while to get there, seems you figured it
out," Quinton said with more cockiness. "Although I only
discovered this recently myself."

I approached Quinton, only a few steps away. Anger
burned inside. "And you didn't tell me!" It took everything in me not to push him into the brick wall.

The older man didn't budge and instead put his hand
on my shoulder. With a gentle warmth, a calm reminded
me of the time in old England, of Constable Green. I
knew it was him long ago, but this made it clear. I stepped
forward, embracing him tightly. Tears trickled on cue—
this time real, not like on the set during my brief stint in
Hollywood. I rest my head on his shoulder, briefly

nestling in to clear the saline. "Sorry for your suit," I laughed.

"Uh, did I miss something?" Mara said from the corner.

Quinton's smile grew wider as he ended the embrace, nodding then patting my back, providing even more comfort.

Alycia shrugged at Mara, then approached Quinton. "So that's why you were looking for him? That's why you wanted to find Hales?"

Quinton wiped a single tear from his eye, a sight that was strange to see in the stoic man before me. "I've been searching for a while." He laughed and walked over to the railing to watch the lights for the first time. "I never imagined you'd find us first. When you traveled back, when you arrived in San Diego, I was almost certain it was you. Tempus was in disarray. Orchid and Lotus plotting on how to handle restoring the timeline and deal with you. At that point, no one even realized that Olivia had traveled. Because technically, you wiped out that timeline too. After the dust settled, it was Melissa who put together the pieces." He paused, giving a much needed summary as he realized my head started to spin. "You survived the initial gunfight with Terrance. Weeks later, when Alycia killed Olivia, her death sent us back. To the night of your vodka release party. However, something changed the second time around. This time, you didn't survive. Then, well, you know the rest." I silently thanked him for spelling it out.

He continued with an oddly apologetic tone, "your seven years of travel took precedence over Olivia's few weeks in a non-existent timeline. She slipped by the radar. And if anyone knew, it was the least of their concern."

"Nothing gets past Melissa," Alycia whispered proudly under her breath.

My tears finally stopped, allowing more focus on the present. Or the past. Or the future. Damn, this was confusing. Another vision erupted in my psyche—Olivia in the old underground amphitheater, sitting next to the bald man, right before she was whisked away, along with any memory of our time together.

"What happened at that ceremony, then?" I crossed my arms, rubbing them more because of the internal chills than the temperature steadily dropping. "You said she could bind to the Council, whatever that meant. Wouldn't they have figured her out then? The man she left with?"

I studied Quinton's face, waiting for a response—only to receive silence and a deep stare. The only noise came from the hum of the lights, a high-pitched buzz accompanied by the clicking of the old electronics turning on and off. I turned to see Alycia waiting as well, intrigued enough by the conversation that she might as well break out the popcorn. Our heads turned to Mara, breaking from the group with a slow saunter through the dirt path toward the flickering signs.

Alycia shifted her weight again, then propped a foot behind on the railing. "Are you going to tell him, or should I?"

Quinton nodded then cleared his throat. "I suppose I should, as you only have part of the story."

I couldn't resist chiming in, even though he appeared ready to spill. "You called him *one of the originals. Like me.*"

I failed horribly at imitating his Mid-Atlantic accent that broke through with certain words.

He rubbed his hands together and looked up at the night sky. I hoped he wouldn't dodge the question as Alycia had earlier. "Your barcode, the symbol on you."

I had a terrible habit of reaching for it whenever it was mentioned. I played it off like I had an itch on my shoulder, but Alycia's smirk told me she saw through the act.

"When I first saw yours, I knew you predated any of us." He shifted his gaze to Mara in the distance, watching her examine the signs with a childlike wonder. "Hers is brand new. More of a rarity these days, but not unheard of." He gestured his hand to Alycia while looking at me. "Most of us are from the same *generation*, I suppose you'd say. One of the few things that carry over in our new lives, along with fragmented memories of the past."

I followed the conversation with my eyes locked on his gesturing hand. Inside his palm, the thick, inches long scar had a faint maroon hue. Did I miss it before? It was neatly tucked between the heart and head lines of the palm—don't ask me how I knew what those meant.

He noticed my stare and made a fist, opening slightly to rub his thumb and index finger together.

"What is that?" I realized the answer as the words came out, lightly slapping my forehead. His *initiation*. The process to join Tempus sure had upgraded over the years.

Quinton nodded with a smirk. "You remember now? Thankfully we've switched to scanning instead of blood-letting."

A sharp laugh escaped Alycia. "I'm glad mine are small enough to cover, not that'd you'd ever see them," she said with a wink. I couldn't believe the killer was flirting with me. I opted not to acknowledge it.

The quiet, ambient noises melted into pure silence as I took a step back. My mind raced with thoughts, finally landing on one which I blurted out loud to no one in particular: "Why haven't they healed then?"

My eyes darted between the two of them, watching their puzzled expressions—Alycia chewing on her bottom lip and Quinton scratching his head.

"So, why haven't they healed over?" I repeated, with a touch of condescension in my voice. "Nothing else from Tempus members leaves scars, right? We fully heal from injuries to each other, even though it hurts like hell." I walked closer to them and spoke with my hands, channeling a TV-detective figuring out the killer at the end of an episode. "Non Tempus members can still hurt us, right? But they wouldn't be the ones cutting, scanning us in. Why are we left with these scars?" I thought of my own, hidden away on my back. I had always assumed it was the product of Terrance's bullets, somehow carrying over from my celebrity life.

Quinton chuckled—a genuine, joyous laugh while he shook his head. Alycia and I traded looks, landing back on Quinton.

"Yeah?" Alycia jumped in, throwing her hands out in confusion. "Care to share?"

He stopped and the smile faded. "I never thought to question it. I just accepted it." He exhaled a deep sigh. "Poor Melissa." He looked over at me with no emotion. "It's how we're going to stop Lucian."

CHAPTER 37

"This must be the place," Mara said, her eyes fixed out the passenger side window.

I was about to reply with a question until I saw the glowing marquee displaying *London Calling* drift into view. An eerie chill swept over like an icy gust of wind. Standing in place of what was once a floral-themed casino was something much different. I turned onto the long, fake cobblestone street leading up to the hotel. The bumpy road was flanked by flickering gas lamps—brushed nickel poles scuffed in an attempt to make them look antique. In the distance, a replica of the London Bridge loomed over the boulevard. Acting as a crosswalk, it guided tourists headed to a New York themed resort. I crept closer to the hotel, passing the out-of-place palm trees to reveal a smaller version of Big Ben on the opposite side. A thick white fog bellowed underneath, defying the current weather of the Vegas night.

The plan had its risks, but other than waiting around we were out of options and had agreed it was our best choice.

"THE ONES WHO LEFT SCARS, they came before us," Quinton had theorized. "I hadn't thought of it until now, but that must be how he was able to hurt, to *kill* Melissa and Pharaoh."

"And you came before him," Alycia added, waving her hand to me. Her confidence was convincing. Almost too much so, but I didn't press it.

The logic made sense, but I didn't want any credit for the discovery. Especially because it meant it was up to me to stop Lucian due to my early generation status, whatever that meant. That is, unless Alycia wanted to reveal her assassin secret, which appeared unlikely.

Neither of them said it outright but the implication was clear. I had to kill him. Even though I had ended plenty of lives a few hundred of years ago in China, the idea of it still made me sick—even with someone as terrible as Lucian. The context was just so different. Back in China, battle was a daily part of life to the point it had been normalized. And being surrounded by death is what led my family to leave Japan anyway. And as for The Butcher, for him I made a special exception. But in my new life, the last decades in America had been relatively safe. It was only until last year that the drama and wild chases took space in my head. Something about the plan seemed wrong. Seemed off. But I couldn't come up with a better solution.

I LOOKED OVER TO MARA, watching her lost in the glamor and elegance of imitation London. The car crawled to a roll in front of the valet booth, itself a reproduction of a small Victorian era townhouse. "I hope you're right about this." Although part of me wished she wasn't.

BACK AT THE ELECTRIC GRAVEYARD, Mara had returned from gazing in the neon lights just in time to answer our next question: How would we find Lucian?

"Guys, this might sound weird, but I need to go." It didn't sound weird to Quinton and Alycia. "I just feel this... draw. It's coming from that direction." The young agent pointed toward the Vegas Strip. "Something is pulling me there."

Quinton gave a short speech about not questioning the power of fate and destiny. And from his private chat with Mara, he'd discovered she was almost as powerful a tracker as Vance.

Alycia was initially against the idea, but Quinton made a convincing argument. "Mara will lead you there, Jay," he said, staring at the high-rise in the distance. "If the theory holds true, Alycia and I will only hold you back. We'll remain back here." I sensed a rare sliver of fear in his voice. For someone as daunting as Quinton, it was uncharacteristic for him to not want a part of the action.

The bigger surprise was Alycia agreeing, causing me to worry even more. "He's right," she said. "We'd only be distractions, if anything. Make sure Mara is safe. *Trust me.*"

I battled the gut reaction to spill her secret right then and there in front of Quinton. Until I read the conflict on her face, the blonde anxiously tense, clenched jaw and shoulders tight. But why wouldn't she offer to come with me? If what she said was true, she too could stop Lucian.

While I trusted their judgment, I got the sense they were both leaving something out. Either way, if the patchwork plan held true, Lucian could only slow me down and couldn't cause any fatal blows—or even orchestrate any from non Tempus members, I had learned from the conversation.

NOW READY FOR THE UNKNOWN, the car stopped in front of the elegant Victorian arched entryway. A man in a bright red tailcoat approached the passenger side, outfit complete with top hat and glistening pocket watch chain. Without hesitation, he pulled the door open, jarring Mara out of her sightseeing. He apologized and helped her from the car like she was royalty, giving the impression it wasn't uncommon to see tourists lost in the aura.

"Sir." A gloved hand tipped the top hat in my direction after the valet approached and graciously accepted my keys. I tried to hide a smirk, noticing his outfit was more suited for the London elite than the working class. I guess they were going for kitschy instead of authenticity —although I doubted they had many guests who had lived through the Victorian-era these days.

"I hope you enjoy your stay with us," the valet added, not giving me a chance to comment on his gear before speeding off.

Another overdressed employee tore open the large gold-rimmed glass door with a slight bow, waving us into the lobby. The smell of expensive oils hit us first, hints of bergamot and clove under the gentle citrus.

"Wow," Mara whispered. "I've passed through Vegas a few times but never actually stepped into the casinos. I feel like I'm in an old English castle. With TVs everywhere."

The theming was all over the place, at least to me. Beautiful, yes. And it must've cost a fortune. I fought to hold back my opinion on the anachronistic nightmare. As someone who lived through the time, the shift from a late 1800s aesthetic to the modern elegance was jarring.

"That chandelier!" Mara walked past the grey brick wall, pausing to glance at the replica artwork, eventually standing directly under the mass of crystal and gold. Her eyes sparked in awe.

"Mr. Hales, I presume," a round bellied man greeted us with a terrible fake British accent. "Welcome to London Calling!" He opened his arms, showcasing the buttons on his tuxedo struggling under the pressure. "Or as your partner calls it, The Whitechapel."

Partner? This was not what I expected. Mara's forehead scrunched, listening from a few feet away, fully alert.

"We've been expecting you," the man added. "You're a touch ahead of *schedule,* though!" I cringed at the attempt to sound as British as possible. Would this have bothered me as much before the memories today?

I hid the displeasure and shock, shooting a giant smile. So much for catching Lucian by surprise, I had to think on my feet. "Of course. I thought I'd drop by for a quick visit."

Keeping it as vague as possible seemed to pay off so far.

"Well, you're more than welcome here anytime! Shall I book you and your," he paused and looked at Mara for a moment, "*friend* a room?" Nosy bastard.

"No, we're just passing through." I needed to figure out what was going on without revealing my hand. "Sweetie, I'd like you to meet someone." I gestured for Mara to meet the man, the ruse working like a charm.

"Goodday, miss. My name is Dominic." He clasped his hands together and bowed. "As a guest of Mr. Hales, I wish to extend the same privileges and honor of being at your service." He attempted to kiss her hand—receiving a laugh instead as she yanked it back.

The woman had the right idea—enough with the pleasantries. I was a VIP, after all. "And what *privileges* would those be?"

Dominic motioned to follow him to the reception desk. "Anything you wish, Mr. Hales! We've been told to be on the lookout for you since our doors opened. It's not every day our angel investor makes a surprise first visit. Shall I notify Mr. Blackwood?"

I did a better job of holding back my laughter than Mara. Ignoring her, I cleared my throat and smoothly shifted gears. Now to sound like an investor. "No, no. Please don't. I'd like to surprise him as well. Is he in?"

"Yes, actually. He arrived from his sabbatical just recently. He's been quite busy today, but I believe he's overseeing the night club construction at the moment. Shall I take you there?"

Sabbatical my ass—Mr. Blackwood was a frozen statue underneath a cemetery for the past year. "Just point me in the right direction. And please clear a table at your finest restaurant for my friend."

The man nodded and gave brief directions. The club was nestled off the game room, just past the stairs leading down to the London Underground monorail stop connecting to the strip. He scurried behind the counter and barked orders at one of the front desk clerks, leaving me and Mara to stand on the beautiful stone floor, surrounded by a constant stream of tourists and guests.

Mara pulled in close for a warm hug. "Don't get any ideas, *sweetie,*" she whispered in my ear. "They might be listening. What the fuck is going on?"

I hugged her back and smiled for the cameras. "Not sure, but hang back. We might still have the jump on him. First sign of danger, find Quinton."

A throat cleared from behind us. We let go to see the portly man smiling ear to ear. "Executive Chef Sutherland is awaiting your arrival, miss. The Regent Room was recently awarded its first Michelin Star. We hope it's to your liking."

Mara scrunched her mouth to the side, pausing to voice disagreement with her eyes. She followed the manager in the opposite direction. I watched as they trotted past the hallway lined with shops displaying elegant jewelry, watches, and British themed clothing stores. Left alone, I stood facing the casino floor, pacing my breath in an attempt to quell the rising anxiety.

I stomped forward, my feet cradled by the plush burgundy carpet. The game room floor buzzed with life. Unmistakable dings of slot machines with their bright flickering lights and the dozens of patrons hoping to score big. The thick smell of tobacco wafted from a gamer sitting alone at a blackjack table playing two hands against the house. The London theme continued into the expanse of betting bliss, with the vaulted ceilings modeled to look like a starry night sky across the pond. In the corners lay old Victorian-looking entryways leading into smaller rooms roped off for the high rollers.

The vibration in my pocket almost went unnoticed, lost to the celebration from an older couple hitting a thousand dollar jackpot. The phone showed one missed call from Alycia. And a voicemail from several minutes ago. *Great.* The reception in the middle of the casino was shit, made worse by the terrible satellites of 2008.

I slunk to a far corner, away from the commotion hoping to hear the message through the ambient casino buzz. The first few seconds of the message were difficult to hear. I ignored another big winner and found an empty row of slots, then put the phone on speaker. Palpitations in my chest increased. I plopped onto a stool and leaned on the machine, listening intently.

"Jay," Alycia's voice was full of urgency. "I don't have much time. Quinton's in the other room. About earlier." A deep sigh. "It had to be you. I'm not sure why, but I just know you had to go there. I didn't want Quinton to know about my abilities, but I promise I'll keep him safe. Be careful." The message cut off, attempts to redial were foiled by a no signal warning. Just the news I needed to hear in this already flimsy mission.

A beautiful redhead zipped by, briefly stealing my focus with her skintight black top and matching grey and black Union Jack skirt. She handled a heavy tray with poise, long strides to ensure safe passage for the multi-colored drinks. Retracing her steps led back to a chic-looking bar. The Jekyll and Hyde had dozens of bottles lining its antique wood shelves, its patrons taking a break for a quick smoke or looking to score another way for the night. Behind rows of beakers, test tubes, and other fake science instruments was a dimly lit hall. At the end, a thick sheet of plastic draped over a high arched entrance. Several stanchions connected by black velvet ropes blocked access—no match against my epic limbo skills.

I drew closer to the plastic barrier until my body froze in place upon spotting the sign. *The Stars Align In 2009. Nyte Sky Coming Soon.* My heart skipped a beat and I swallowed hard. I glanced back, studying the bustling casino floor. It looked so different, although the layout remained the same. This was no coincidence—I was standing at the future site of the vodka release party—the site of my assassination. An air-conditioned breeze floated by carrying the scent of jasmine and citrus, briefly lifting the plastic.

The break offered a quick preview of the faintly lit, unfinished nightclub. The inside was different from what I remembered in 2014. As with the casino, the structure remained the same underneath the aesthetic changes. A large bar sat unfinished at one end of the club. Sitting opposite it were rows of booths, tarped over and covered with plastic sheets bearing a thick layer of sawdust. Above, several large platforms appeared almost completed.

A voice burrowed out deep within my brain. *"Ladies and gentlemen, the man of the hour, Mr. Jay Hagaki!"* A flicker of light shot across my eyes with a sharp pang, with it the memory of a woman dancing atop the platform. Olivia.

I swept the plastic aside and stepped onto the cardboard-lined floor, the barrier struggling to protect the rich, dark marble underneath. An assault of applause echoed as a vision of a packed club flashed by. A much older Paul Washington approached. His actor persona, Paul Jackson, raising a glass to toast the celebrity of the night.

A haphazardly placed canvas bag interrupted my stroll through memory lane. Tumbling forward to the floor, I met the various tools I knocked over, clanking onto unprotected tile. I couldn't help but laugh, noticing the fall had chipped a piece of the brand new expensive marble. Dusting myself off, I rose, eyeing a staircase leading up to the VIP area and manager's office. My skin prickled, another chilly wave washing over me despite the lack of any air circulation in the stagnant club.

With heavy feet, I inched closer to the stairs, slowed by more memories of the fatal night. After each step up toward the black, closed door, more images danced by: A rude awakening from smelling salts in a limo. Punching my manager, Julio. The elaborate *Hagaki Vodka* display. Amber, the flirtatious nightclub owner.

I ran both hands over my eyes, the short massage ending after the pain warned I had pushed too hard.

An uncomfortable sensation suddenly pressed into my torso. *"Take my gun,"* Alycia had said earlier, handing over the weapon I somehow instantly recognized as a Glock. *"For Lucian."* Hesitantly accepting, the gun found its way to my waistline.

Palm pressed on the door, my fingers paused. Maybe there's nothing waiting? But the parallels were eerie, too similar. Armed, ready to face my future, in the same place where it all started.

The door swung open revealing an empty office. Unfurnished. No desk, couches, or chairs greeted me. On the back wall, a glass sliding door was taped with thin brown paper blocking the view of the yet-to-be constructed balcony overlook. I felt the relief first, my shoulders dropping as the tension faded. The disappointment came next, taking a few steps forward, wondering why Mara had been drawn here.

I closed my eyes and inhaled the fragrant sheetrock, lumber, and assorted chemicals wafting from the new construction. My eyelids opened, now to the room filled with furniture. The window now magically restored, lights flashed from the nightclub below synchronized to the loud bass thumps. Terrance Stewart, vice president of Paradise Records, paced behind a desk. His words incoherent, sounding like Charlie Brown's teacher in the Red

Room from Twin Peaks. Next to him stood my agent Julio, peering back with an equally annoying grin.

Terrance's arm rose, his gun floating upward pointed in my direction. Pieces of glass exploded on the ground at my side. I stepped forward as the overhead lights flickered, turning to face the front of the room and exposing my back to the attackers. Frozen in stillness, I faced an older, grizzled version of myself. In his eyes, a hurricane of emotion stirred. Fear. Anger.

"We need to go back, further." Olivia stood near the door. Her words echoed through the room as she drew her hand away from the light switch.

A different emotion appeared in the almost thirty-something celebrity Hagaki's eyes: an understanding calm.

Olivia approached him from behind, unfettered by the frozen world around her. Wrapping her hands around the older Hagaki, the tight embrace held his arms in place. Olivia paused, looking over his shoulder and directly in my direction. My heart fluttered and skipped a series of beats. I almost missed the subtle change in her expression—the corner of her mouth ever so slightly curving into a smile. And time resumed.

Explosions clanged off the walls, accompanied by flashes of gold and white. On the floor, patches of red developed on the celebrity's shirt before the colors swirled together and faded away.

Stillness enveloped while the light dimmed in the empty office. I was alone again. The only thumping coming from my heart struggling to remain in my chest. *That look.* She couldn't have seen me, could she?

Dazed, I walked to the end of the office and tore the

paper covering the window. The nightclub was unchanged. Dark and empty. Now with an overhead view, I surveyed the work in progress, various tools and dangerous looking equipment scattered across the dance floor.

"Another chance... I think I tried to fix it... I tried to warn you—" Her words flowed into the theory-filled conversation with Quinton, all the pieces starting to sink into place.

I laughed out loud and spoke to the empty club. "She didn't try to warn me—"

"She made sure you died," the voice interrupted from behind.

Mara shuffled in from the doorway, her arms pulled back tight, hands bound behind for the second time today. Specks of red ruined her shirt from the small gash on her temple, already beginning to dry. A thick layer of tape covered her mouth, the only talking coming from her eyes darting around the room. I imagined her federal agent training kicking in—calculating the chances of survival and looking for an escape.

Lucian towered behind, the clack of his shiny black dress shoes echoing with every step. Even in the dim light, blinding flashes of silver beamed off his cufflinks. The jewelry matched the color of his wavy hair, grey strands extending to the shoulders of an expensive black tuxedo.

Lanky alabaster fingers pressed into the captive, sending her stumbling forward. The agent quickly caught her balance, showcasing impressive core strength.

"That's far enough," he said, his skeletal hand gripping Mara's gun, hovering mere feet from her back.

Motionless, I stood with my back to the newly uncovered sliding window. Even with all my experience in battle, being lost in the memory had sapped any instinct, leaving me defenseless. For at least the second time today, Lucian had passed on the opportunity to make use of my vulnerability. I doubted he was a man of honor, leading me to believe Quinton was right—Lucian couldn't kill me. I smirked at the thought, turning into a short laugh.

From behind Mara's shielding, Lucian's voice emerged. "I can appreciate a good joke. But alas, the only humor here is the irony of your death in the same place you had once eluded it." His voice had a deeper, raspy quality I hadn't noticed the first time we met, although our meeting had been so brief and chaotic I barely recognized him.

Despite the situation, Mara's face didn't show fear. Instead, her eyes continually shifted to my left, flashing brief, intentional squints. Was she signaling something? Morse code maybe, but I figured that only worked in the movies. Fingers running through my beard, I tugged at the strands while I stalled to come up with a plan. I could try to shoot him, knowing I'd survive even if he landed some shots on me. Mara complicated that plan—a hit from me or Lucian *might* be fatal and not something I wanted to risk. I took a confident step forward. Maybe I could get under his skin and find out what he knew. It seemed to work with The Butcher. "What do you know about Olivia?"

He hesitated before answering, lip scrunching to the corner of his face. "An unforeseen complication." His expression returned to the pompous asshole that first strolled in. "We hadn't realized your sweet Olivia was one of us."

We.

Had Alycia been lying all along? Or was she trying to come clean just minutes ago on the phone? She admitted to killing Olivia in that future, but claimed not to remember why and seemed genuinely remorseful. A bead of sweat dripped down Mara's eyebrow, the first signs of apprehension. *Just a little longer*—the message I tried to send with my eyes. Saving her would have to come after the answers.

I carefully crossed my arms making no sudden movements. "You and Alycia have had it out for me from the beginning, huh?"

Lucian's head cocked back slightly with a chuckle. "Alycia? Excellent at her job. And following orders." I caught the slightest waver of the heavy pistol in his hand. Unless the suit was hiding some muscle, his thin frame couldn't hold that position forever. "She's freed as well?" A quick pause of surprise before he continued. "You have bigger problems than the assassin."

Mara shifted her weight to the other leg. The well-dressed asshole stepped closer, pushing the pistol harder to her spine. Her back tightened and shot upwards from the pressure and shock, more glimmers of fear sinking in.

"This will be over soon, dear. At least for you." His tone was eerily calming, parental. He seemed to enjoy causing pain. Memories of the sadistic Butcher of Whitechapel crossed my mind. *No, it couldn't be.*

And I was running out of options. If Lucian killed her now, would the day reset again? Even with her being scanned in and finally crossing into the next day, I wasn't confident about placing that bet. "What's with the creepy villain standoff? You could have killed me instead of taking Vance."

Embracing the word *creepy,* his tongue slithered out and licked the top of his lip. "I would be lying if I said this didn't amuse me, but it's an excellent bonus, I suppose."

I tilted my head. "I don't follow."

"You took seven long years from me. Years I spent solidifying my position in Tempus. Seeing you suffer *and* regaining my status, well, he's given me quite the gift. Not to mention bringing me out of that crypt." The tall man studied my puzzled expression before continuing. "I wish I could claim credit for all of this. He built this *for you.* And he's been waiting for oh, *such a very long time.* You're only alive right now because he wants it that way. Her though?"

He backed away and lowered the gun. A bright light swallowed the room while my ears rang in pain.

CHAPTER 40

I turned toward the noise, seeing one of the large wooden double doors slam shut. A gust of stale, humid air tickled my nose. I searched the mahogany walled room, eyes temporarily blinded by the sun streaming through the breaks in the windows. The dusty stained glass created beautiful rays of color on the pews and front of the chapel. The front showed no discernible denomination or religious markings, only a small wooden lectern worn by years of neglect. Now adjusted to the light, more signs of disrepair were evident —mold on the walls, broken seating, and patches of sunlight leaking from holes in the tall ceiling. I continued to scan the room for any signs of life, drifting over to the right. A brown leather glove slapped down onto my shoulder, shock causing breath to escape in a sharp huff.

"Eyes forward," the voice ordered. I couldn't place a face to the mysterious, heavy Spanish accent—contrasting the uncomfortable, familiar shiver it sent down my spine.

My eyes landed on a singular brick, focusing on the slight yellowish discoloration causing it to stand out from the brown and red wall.

"You're a hard man to find, Hales." The hand tightened before it released, coinciding with the sound of the man settling in the pew behind. Hot breath clawed at the nape of my neck. "Or is it Green?"

With a deep inhale, I fought the urge to turn my head, wishing I knew the identity of the speaker. "Who are you?"

The guest whistled a faint, high-pitched series of notes before continuing, a distinct jingle that seemed vaguely familiar. "I hoped you'd remember by now, *Hagaki*." My name had a ghostly echo that rang throughout the derelict sanctuary. "Clever little ruse using the fool's body. Too bad I didn't sense your life flicker out, like it will in a few hours."

The old wooden seat creaked as the hot breath intensified behind. "I've got nothing but time, old friend."

The pain came in waves, searing deep within my shoulder and extending to my fingertips. I emptied my lungs, exhaling air I didn't know was inside. My eyes rolled back into their sockets, slight beams of light fought to creep into view. I tried to move my right arm and realized it was limp, the rest of my body agreeing with mutiny, leaving me stuck to the pew. Whatever had entered my body was removed in a swift motion, leaving a wet trail accumulating in its place.

Sound swirled as the assailant's boots echoed to the front of the old church. "The poison is slow. And painful."

My throat began to pulsate and swell. I fought for air in short gasps and found the strength to speak, managing only one word. "Whyyy—" The airway snapped closed, leaving room for what little oxygen it could handle. My eyelids trembled, eyes eventually sinking down. I focused on the man through the blurry vision, finding him standing off to the side. Every muscle rejected the commands to move—panic adding to the pain coursing within.

"Why?" the shadow said, seething with anger as it jolted into view mere inches from my face. "Because you have what I never will." Vision returned in brief bursts, vacillating between clarity and an undesirable mess. That horrible smile—I had seen it before. Not in this form, not in this lifetime. "You remember," he said, the smile growing with a sick pleasure.

The burning in my lungs intensified with every short breath. The poison was working its way fast through each nerve, traveling through my spine one disc at a time. With my remaining energy, I commanded the full force of muscles to grab the man—causing only my ring and pinky fingers to flicker.

"Keep trying," the voice said.

My head dropped to the side, spine unable to support the weight. While the world smeared into a haze of color, the blurry shadow stepped away and disappeared out of sight.

The voice trailed as it drifted further behind. "And as long as you do, I am going to keep finding you and make your existence hell."

The heavy door slammed shut, leaving me paralyzed in fear and pain.

CHAPTER 41

Mara dropped to a knee then fell to the side as a trickle of blood oozed from her ankle. I followed the aim of my gun, finding it locked on Lucian mirroring the same. I didn't fire—the yearning to understand why holding back my trigger finger.

Another blast rattled my skull. I would have loved to say I spun away from the bullet, dodging it in some elaborate movement. Instead, I flinched at the explosion and again at the glass shattering behind. In the millisecond I glanced down at Mara, the vengeful creep's bullet cut through my fingers. I dropped the pistol, waving my hand in hopes it would stop the searing pain. It didn't. After realizing what happened, I made a fist to stop the blood droplets raining on the floor.

The shooter aimed his pistol back at Mara. No change in emotion. "Arms up. Move again, and it's her other leg," the harsh voice ordered.

I raised both arms above my head. A thin stream of blood pooled from the mangled palm, flowing down my forearm causing it to twitch.

Lucian drew a step closer, his eyes never leaving mine. "So ungrateful. Not appreciating this gift. He thought it would be a nice reminder." He waved the gun as he spoke, making sure to keep my torso in this path. "Starting to bring back a few for me, too." I almost missed the second flinch of his elbow. He was stalling but couldn't hold on much longer.

Mara wriggled in pain beneath the towering gunman. Her bound hands struggled, failing to reach her injured leg.

"I'm going to give you a choice," his words slithered out. "Stay put until he arrives and her death will be quick. Try any heroics and I'll make sure it's slow and painful."

He. Every mention brought a series of nameless faces flashing across my mind until landing on one: the executioner at the old church. The face cleared, focusing as a layer of haze lifted. The light brown complexion of a wrinkled, unkempt bearded face. A pain in my temples followed the next vision: a quick glance, a different face. The bald man at the ceremony last year. The first and last time I saw him, taking Olivia away. The man Quinton referred to as an original. Another piece clicked into the puzzle, borders not yet defined making it seem endless.

Lucian rolled his shoulder, showing even more signs of fatigue despite the gun being lowered and focused on Mara. His eyes narrowed after realizing I caught the movement. If I rushed him now, would I be faster than the older man? And even if he couldn't kill me, the bullets would tear through, leaving me a sitting duck as I healed while *He* made his way here. I snuck a final glance at the ground, catching the spikey haired woman writhing about, crawling closer to the gunman. If I do nothing, she would be dead either way—in the words of the King, *It's Now or Never*.

My arms began a slow descent from above with a well timed wink across the room. Lucian's attempt to protest was cut short, turning the beginning of his command into a howl of pain. His left leg buckled from the glass shard Mara lodged into his calf. I launched forward, grabbing his arm to follow with a nasty punch to his chest. With a loud exhale he dropped the pistol, the weapon joining my gun and the glass scattered below.

Despite his appearance, I had misjudged his strength. He fought back with a well-timed elbow to my nose, causing me to stumble backward and smell iron. From his inner pocket, a medium blade joined the fight. I narrowly dodged the first two slashes. Third was the charm for the attacker as I slipped on some glass, leaving myself open—literally. The slice tore across my abdomen and sent me further back. I won the fight to stay upright with help from the railing, narrowly toppling out the window overlooking the dance floor. Closing the distance quickly, the spry old man sprang forward blade first, piercing just shy of my heart. I winced, fighting through the fiery, wet agony spilling down my chest.

Inches away, we locked eyes. Through the pulsating misery, he projected flickers of chaos forcing me into a new battle—fighting a spiraling descent into his madness. Our thoughts twisted into one—fear and a sickly inhuman pleasure. His mind relished in the dominance while telegraphing the next thought, digging the blade deeper with both hands. The millisecond warning was all I needed.

Pushing away the psychic horrors, I leveraged my back against the windowsill, delivering a swift kick to his injured leg. His hands left the blade as he slipped backward and doubled over. Wasting no time, he rose upright, brushing off the attack like a robot re-energized. With an eerie smile he paused, enjoying my struggle, watching the failed attempts to reach the protruding blade.

The shots rang out in quick succession. Three bullets pierced his chest from the floor behind, one tearing out, whizzing by my ear. Stumbling forward in shock, he reached out to me, his hands trembling. Before he could correct his balance, I used his own momentum and grabbed onto the killer's tuxedo. With one forceful pull, I leaned far out the broken window. Gravity, momentum, and a few bullets on my side, we both tumbled down, out onto the nightclub below.

As the metallic cracks echoed through the room, a dense cloud of gypsum and silica particles diffused into the air. The specs of dust danced in the dim fluorescent lights, giving the appearance of a winter snowfall. With only eyes moving, I laid limp, cradled in numbness. Even with plenty of experience in Tempus, my years of humble humanity made it difficult to believe I could survive the gunshots, stabbings, and falls. The lack of sensation brought a very real fear—could this be it? Learning Alycia's secret and the damn new generation rules made it confusing.

"Wiggle your toes." A clatter echoed before Mara's slender silhouette cut through the dust. "Can you feel your toes?" The voice began to sync up to the angelic form hovering above, complete with her own halo of light from the ceiling.

The numbness turned into thousands of pins pricking at my feet, like spiders quickly crawling their way up my spine then into my face. I lurched my body forward, finding I had landed squarely in one of the booths. A thick bundle of burlap blankets helped cushion the fall on the unforgiving marble table. Several feet away, the long tuxedoed man lay face up, bent inhumanly backwards over a heavy steel shop light. A piece of bloodied metal poked out from his stomach, joining the bullet holes in his chest. I forced my eyes away from the gory scene of organs forcefully evacuated out from his torso.

"Hey, don't move your head!" The soft hand grabbed my neck and eased me lower.

My eyes wept, turning Mara's dusty body into a mosaic of watercolors. "You look like shit," I said, hoping it came with a smile before the world turned to black.

DESPITE BEING ABOUT AN HOUR AWAY, I opted to see Dr. Shen—as always, the fewer people involved, the better. Or at least that's what Quinton informed the doctor I had mumbled between my bouts of lucidity.

"Good call," Shen said with a wink. "I'm still not too keen about Blake roaming freely after what happened, but hey, what do I know?" She scribbled on a clipboard and dropped it at the foot of my bed before heading for the exit. As the door closed behind her, I caught a glimpse of Alycia talking to Mara's partner in the hall.

"Welcome back to the land of the living," Quinton said. His fingers wrapped around the bedrail, showing off a variety of rings I never noticed. Each had a cryptic insignia that glittered under the overhead lighting, a reminder of the secret groups from countless historical documentaries. "Mara is healing well. Vance is meeting with her now." The fingers tapped across the steel bar. "You gave us quite the scare."

I coughed out a laugh that came with a sharp pain in my lower abdomen. After massaging my belly, I sat up, realizing I wasn't in a neck brace. Thoughts felt delayed, slowed from whatever chemicals flowed from the IV bags into my veins.

"Had you worried, huh?" My words came out slurred.

His lip trembled before beaming a grin. "Figure of speech, of course. We knew you'd pull through." The nodding seemed overly excessive, too eager.

I raised an eyebrow at the grey-haired man, his reaction triggering a thought I pushed aside earlier. After a chortle of my own, I attempted to cross my arms until the IV line pulled taut. "There's something I've been wondering." A noticeable gulp of air passed through Quinton's throat. "Back at the museum. You sent me after Lucian because of my mark, because I'm an *original*, you claim." The wince returned on the man's face, like he bit into a sour lemon. One so sour he took another step back and remained silent until I continued. "I had some time in my coma-daze to wonder. Just what *generation* were Melissa and Pharaoh?"

The new Tempus leader only nodded, hints of shame across his face upon knowing where the conversation was headed.

I continued the gentle prodding. "And remember last year in the cemetery when Lucian shot you, *brother*?"

"Why, why yes. When I jumped in front of his bullets to save your life, if I remember correctly!"

Even though I knew the answers to the questions, I

was livid, realizing the plan was flawed from the beginning. He was lucky—if it weren't for the calming medications sedating my words, Quinton would have heard more than this monotone inquisition. "And yet you survived. You knew Lucian couldn't kill you. Just as he couldn't have killed the others. Either he received magic powers in the last year or—"

The door behind him swung open. Alycia stomped in sarcastically chipper, baring her gleaming white teeth. "I straightened everything out. The world is back in the dark like it *should* have been." That last part was directed at me, bits of fire in her voice. Even in a hospital bed, I couldn't get a break. "What did I miss?"

Quinton cleared his throat after a nervous laugh. I cut him off before he was about to talk. "I was just asking how you two knew Lucian was behind all this."

"Oh," Alycia said casually. "We didn't."

Quinton slapped his forehead, then turned to her. "You could have some tact!"

I pushed my head into the soft hug of the pillows. When I looked back, Alycia was shrugging. "It worked, didn't it? Quinton and I argued about it until Mara called to come get you."

The missed phone call. The cryptic voicemail. So it was the assassin's guilty conscience breaking through to give me a warning.

"I'm sorry, Jay." His face was dressed in guilt. "I knew you could stop him. The rest, I'm not entirely sure. I still believe you were safe."

Alycia approached the railing, leaning down to look me over. "I'll be direct. To answer your question, no, we don't think Lucian killed them. He's from our generation." She leaned in close with a hushed tone only I could hear, "and not like me." She stood back and continued after confirming Quinton had missed the secret whisper. "He wasn't alone. There must be another." She let go of the bar and stood straight, clenching her jaw in a painful expression before continuing. "Someone from long ago."

My eyes widened. Leaning forward, I could feel each disc shift as my spine elongated. Foggy thoughts cleared, turning into a singular newfound focus. Muscles tightened, ready for battle. An urge to move, to fight, to attack —to kill Lucian's puppeteer. I thrashed against the rails as a new, urgent beeping added to the chaos.

"Woah there!" Alycia tapped a button on the machine above. "You can't just start yanking things out. Wait for the nurse!"

My eyes frantically searched the room. The world was unsafe. Adrenaline flowed freely, heightening every sensation.

Quinton joined Alycia to flank me on the other side of the bed with a reassuring but forceful hand. "Breathe."

EPILOGUE

"Breathe. You are going to be alright."

I looked for the voice but all I saw was black. My head felt heavy like my spine was ready to collapse.

"I'm taking off the wrapping. Open your eyes. Slowly." The voice's pitch shifted, a low baritone morphing into an octave so high it didn't seem human.

I winced in pain, snapping my eyelids tight. Even as the sun set, the burning light caused tears to stream down my face making the brilliant star appear cyan. At least that's what made the most sense.

"Slowly," the ethereal voice repeated with a jovial inflection.

I wiped away the tears, exposing beautiful stretches of open land. The lush green rolling hills of the Chinese countryside. My body became weightless causing me to lose balance upon standing. Strong, boney hands pulled me tight and upright.

"You don't listen well, do you?" A hearty laugh boomed from an invisible crowd of dozens before stopping abruptly as the hold released.

A sharp throb stabbed both ears, hot and wet. The hilly fields turned gold then flickered purple before settling back into a natural mossy green. I ran a hand up to the pain, returning it to find warm, red, glistening fingers.

"I apologize for that," the warbled words sounded sincere.

I scanned the surroundings, finding I was alone on the dirt road leading from my village. "What happened?" I took a step forward, now feeling the effects of gravity along with the weight of the heavy imperial armor.

The pause lingered in the wind before the voice finally continued. "We've returned one week before your death. It's time for your second chance. But it comes at a cost."

Electricity entered my shoulder, sucking all air from my lungs.

～

DARKNESS. A lamp clicked on from the nightstand, gently illuminating the room.

"The dream again?" whispered the soft British voice.

I turned to find Alycia sitting upright against the headboard, brushing long, dark red locks away from her sleepy eyes. She pulled a hair tie off her wrist and fixed the disheveled strands up in a ponytail, revealing a Coldplay shirt—their 2011 tour.

A bead of sweat dripped from my cheek onto the comforter. I wiped my face and leaned forward, taking slow, measured breaths like we'd been practicing for the past few months.

"We cremated the bastard," she said, repeating the nightmare-drill we created together. "And the ghost never came. And he'll never come." Her hand caressed my neck. "We are safe."

Her words were reassuring, even though I started doubting the authenticity after the dozen or so times I heard them. That was my insecurity. I felt guilty for waking her so often, especially on our romantic getaway. I looked out the giant glossy windows, staring into a serene expanse of ocean gently lapping on the sandy beach. The indigo morning sky further calmed my pulsating nerves, the slightest hint of sunset kissing a palm tree swaying next to the cabana.

"We are safe," she repeated.

I fought the urge to argue like I had the last time. She was being the forever optimist as usual—something that surprised me to find in the Tempus assassin. Deep down, I worried she had no way of truly knowing. But she was right. The ghost, as we called him, never came. He vanished, like the mysterious USB drive Dr. Chen removed from my body.

Making things more difficult, both Alycia and Quinton's memories were spotty. While Quinton remembered most of our dealings with The Butcher, he hit a block whenever trying to recall the man stalking me from afar and his attempts to find me. And Alycia denied ever knowing a past life in Whitechapel, leading me to wonder just who Sofie was. It had to be her or was my memory at fault?

I inhaled deeply, the light salty scent of warm ocean air creeping in. I paused, debating if I should tell her the dream was new. At least the other one had become predictable. "I'm fine," I said, looking around the large suite to adjust to the present. "I'm sorry. I thought I'd sleep better in paradise."

The soft lips left a tingle on my cheek. "It's okay, I have snorkeling in two hours anyway." She rolled from the bed and started for the bathroom. "Are you sure you don't want to join me? You still owe me a few more years, *asshole*." She blew a kiss and walked away.

I enjoyed a solid half hour watching the beach come to life in the sun, sipping my dark, bitter coffee on the balcony. Alycia had left for her snorkeling class, looking cute as ever in the USA flag bikini she wore ironically, after my cringey joke gift. The last few years were a blur and shockingly *normal*. After killing Lucian and racing from the hospital, I spent a year in fear, looking over my shoulder—and searching for Olivia. Any hint of her disappeared to the point I wondered if she ever even existed. Quinton assured me I hadn't fabricated her, although sometimes I wish I had.

Time and exhaustion eventually gave way, moving on at a snail's pace. It helped that Tempus was finally quiet —at times feeling like a routine part-time gig—until my night job, that is. I leaned forward after the last swig of joe, then traced my finger around the small jewelry box. Aly pulled me out of something darker than the cold brew stuck to the bottom of my cup. Why not join the rest of the masses and tie the knot?

I sauntered back into the suite with a soft grin, filled with purpose and caffeine. My hip accidentally bumped the desk, jostling the mouse and lighting up my MacBook. *Memoirs of Lyrical Man* stared back from Google Drive. Surprisingly, labeling it as fiction got around any Tempus secrecy rules. I thought it was ready for the public, but the publisher said it was too hard to follow and wasn't keen on how I ordered the events. I was close to telling them to shove it. I closed the laptop and changed into my swim trunks, hoping I'd catch Alycia by the pool.

With the sun's rays now beaming down, the poolside started to fill in. Luckily, I found an empty lounger near the hottub. A sharp pinch stung my shoulder, causing me to swat the pain without thought. Even a five-star resort can't stop the insects, I guess.

After a few minutes of watching the waves, the heat seemed to intensify—my throat beckoning for the water bottle just within arms reach. My shoulder pulsated again, a warmth developing like a sudden sunburn. As I extended my hand, waves of nausea washed over. I swiped at the bottle, completely missing and falling hard onto the wet stone, shattering my sunglasses in the process.

As I attempted to reorient myself from upside down, a pair of muscular legs wrapped in tight business attire clicked in front of me.

"Miss me inspector?" Olivia said, not wasting a moment before adding urgency in her voice. "Get up Hales, he's on his way."

A BIG THANKS

Thank you so much for reading my second novel. A lot of love and time went into its creation. Many thanks go to my beta readers, especially Brion <3.

As an indie author, I appreciate any and all of your support. Reviews really make a difference. So if you loved this, consider dropping a few words on Amazon or Goodreads, telling a friend, sharing on socials, and/or giving me a like here or there.

There's more to this story to come, along with a few other tales. So keep a lookout. And for all the latest updates and freebies, check out my newsletter:

> Signup: www.steventemplar.com/news